HarperFestival is an imprint of HarperCollins Publishers.

© 2009 Ilion Animation Studios, HandMade Films International & A3 Films.
Planet 51™ and all related characters, places, names and other indicia are trademarks of Ilion Studios, S.L.,
HandMade Films International Limited & A3 Films S.L. All rights reserved.
Printed in the United States of America.
No part of this book may be used or reproduced in any manner whatsoever without written
permission except in the case of brief quotations embodied in critical articles and reviews.
For information address HarperCollins Children's Books,
a division of HarperCollins Publishers, 10 East 53rd Street, New York, NY 10022.
www.harpercollinschildrens.com
Library of Congress catalog card number: 2009932798
ISBN 978-0-06-184419-5
09 10 11 12 13   LP/CW   10 9 8 7 6 5 4 3 2 1
❖
First Edition

PLANET 51

THE JUNIOR NOVEL

By J. E. Bright

HARPER FESTIVAL
An Imprint of HarperCollinsPublishers

Chapter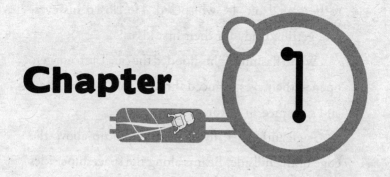

On a quiet road near a hillside forest, a teenage couple sat close together in the front seat of a parked car. The only light came from the weak glow of the dashboard radio. The teenagers could see only each other's silhouette.

"I've never gone parking before," the girl admitted with a nervous giggle. "I'm not that kind of girl."

The guy smiled, and squeezed the girl's hand gently. "I'm not the kind of guy who would go with that kind of girl."

"Aw, that's so sweet." The girl sighed. "I think." She closed her eyes and puckered up her lips.

The teenage boy leaned closer. "There's nothing

to be scared of," he whispered. He closed his eyes, too, getting ready for their first kiss.

Weird flashing lights flooded the car. The teenagers opened their eyes, glanced through the back window, and screamed in terror.

A gigantic alien flying saucer rose up above the edge of the hillside. Beams along the spaceship's sides shined like giant flashlights through the misty night.

"I knew this would happen if we kissed!" the teenage girl screamed.

The boy shouted in terror, then he shifted the car into gear and raced down the dark road.

The alien ship shot sizzling lasers out of its base at the escaping car.

The teenagers screamed again, and the car weaved crazily on the road as the boy tried to dodge the dangerous blasts.

The spaceship soared after the car, closing in. But then the car suddenly halted—it had reached an overlook, the end of the road. The flying saucer couldn't stop that quickly, and overshot its prey. The alien craft had to circle back in the air, lowering itself toward the car. It took careful aim with its lasers, preparing to strike—

Blam!

Something had shot the flying saucer! The spaceship teetered in the air, before crashing into the side of the hill, sliding down toward the base of the cliff.

Down below, dozens of soldiers with tanks and big guns waited, ready to battle the alien attacker.

"Good shot!" a general called out.

With tendrils of smoke streaming out of it, the huge alien spacecraft lay still where it had landed. All the soldiers aimed their weapons at the flying saucer's main hatch.

The hatch slowly opened, and a hideous, one-eyed creature stepped out onto the ramp. He waved tentacle-like arms above his misshapen head.

"General," a military aide shouted, "I think he is surrendering!"

That's when the alien started shooting death rays at the soldiers from his single eye. The deadly beam blasted everything it hit into tiny particles.

"Fire at will!" the general hollered.

The soldiers shot at the alien all at once, but the creature cleared the space around him with his eye beam. The alien summoned a full fleet of alien ships. Hundreds of flying saucers swarmed toward the soldiers, firing their lasers. But the soldiers fired back with everything they had. The scene erupted into total, chaotic war.

A near miss with one laser knocked off the general's helmet.

The two antennae on the general's head sprang free, poking out of a tangle of squishy-looking hair. He had long, pointy ears, and almost no nose at all.

"Keep firing!" the general ordered, putting his helmet back on. "Kill every last alien!"

In the movie theater where the science-fiction film was playing, the crowd cheered the general's orders. Everyone in the audience also had squishy hair, short antennae, and almost no nose. They all had greenish skin and only four fingers. Most of them were kids and teenagers, enjoying a rowdy matinee. All of them were wearing 3-D glasses, and they jumped out of their seats every time an explosion shook the oval screen or a flying saucer swooped toward the camera.

In the middle of the front row, a nine-year-old boy named Eckle sat on the edge of his seat, munching popcorn as he gazed up at the screen. Eckle's pointed, greenish yellow ears stuck out from the sides of his head, giving him an impish look. His red baseball cap was backward on his head, the strap pressing against his antennae. He was completely engrossed in the film—especially when the aliens used ray guns to turn people into zombies.

Someone suddenly pulled off Eckle's 3-D glasses. "Hey!" he protested, but his face sagged when he saw his mother glaring down at him.

"Resistance is futile!" an alien on the screen hollered.

Eckle's mother grabbed him by one antenna and dragged him out of the theater and into the lobby.

"What did I tell you about these kinds of movies?" Eckle's mother scolded. Posters all around the lobby advertised movies with titles such as *Humaniacs III* and *The Beast with Ten Fingers*.

"It was almost over," Eckle grumbled, as his mother dragged him outside onto Main Street. The sky was overcast with dark clouds—it was going to rain soon. The stores along the street were made of brick and wood, with bright striped awnings. Most of the buildings were round, with domes for roofs. Eckle's mother didn't let go of his antenna as she led him toward the crosswalk, where a woman was waiting with her hover stroller.

After a few floating, bubble-shaped cars had passed, the policeman directing traffic motioned for them all to cross the street. As Eckle passed the stroller, the cop, Police Chief Gorloc, leaned over to the baby inside. It was just a big egg in the seat.

"Gootchie-gootchie-goo!" Chief Gorloc cooed, tickling the egg. He then glanced up and smiled at the woman with the stroller. "He looks just like his father!"

Eckle's mother pulled him over to their car just as the clouds above rumbled. A street sweeper near the car let out a sigh as small rocks started raining down.

"I hate the rain!" the sweeper complained, cleaning up the bouncing rocks with his broom. One rock beaned him on the head. "Ouch!"

Eckle and his mother got in the car and rode to the observatory on the hill above Main Street, where she halted abruptly outside a building with a big white dome.

"Just wait until your father hears about this," Eckle's mother said.

"But it's not a mandatory field trip," Eckle whined. "It's *so* boring!"

They got out of the car and his mother reached over and grabbed his antenna, dragging him inside the observatory to the planetarium, where his class was.

The circular planetarium was dark, and filled with Eckle's classmates, who were all gazing up at the projected stars on the ceiling. In the middle of the room was a raised platform, where a star projector and an operator stood. Around the platform were little dangling mobiles of model planets and stars.

Eckle knew the operator—he was a sixteen-year-old named Lem who lived in the house next door to Eckle's family.

"Space!" Lem announced excitedly. "A universe of mystery." Lem held up a textbook entitled *Our Small, Small World* and waved it in front of him. "Well, today the mystery will be unveiled. Thanks to science, we now know the universe is nearly five hundred miles long. It contains—you're not going to believe this—more than one thousand stars!"

A few kids yawned in boredom.

Eckle pushed his way through the crowd toward the platform. On the other side of the projector, he spotted an older man taking notes on a clipboard. Eckle bit his lip—he knew that the older guy was the planetarium curator, who was judging Lem's performance.

"*Psst!*" someone hissed from the other side of Lem. Both Eckle and Lem turned to look, and saw a friend of Lem's named Skiff sitting casually in one of the seats. Skiff was geeky and a little weird. He had a big, round bald head and braces on his top teeth, but Eckle knew that he could always be counted on for some entertaining ideas about aliens.

Skiff gave Lem a thumbs-up, motioning for him to keep going with his presentation. "C'mon, Lem!" Skiff whispered loudly. "Liven it up!"

Lem took a deep breath, and picked up a slide. For a second, he couldn't get the slide into the right slot on the projector, but finally an image of their planet appeared on the ceiling dome.

"The only known intelligent life is right here on our planet," Lem announced.

Lem must have put the slide in wrong, because the square of film caught fire.

"No, please," Lem groaned, fumbling to pull out the burning slide. "Not today."

Before Lem could remove the slide, the image on the ceiling was swallowed up in flickering flames. It made their planet look like it was being destroyed.

The kids in the audience let out a terrified moan, and some screamed or started sobbing.

"What was that?" one boy gasped.

Eckle jumped up onto the edge of the platform. "That's our planet after the attack of the Humaniacs!"

he yelled. "They're going to eat our brains for dinner!"

Eckle smiled as the kids freaked out.

"Is that true?" someone screeched.

Lem raised his hands, trying to calm the crowd. "Everyone, please!" he called out. "That's ridiculous!"

"Totally ridiculous," said Skiff, standing up. "C'mon, aliens don't eat brains for dinner. They eat brains for breakfast, with cereal and milk."

One boy in the crowd clutched his stomach, grossed out by Skiff's announcement. His face turned pale.

"For dinner," Skiff continued, "aliens eat organs and eyeballs."

The boy threw up.

The curator shook his head, and wrote another note on his clipboard. Eckle didn't think Lem was getting a good grade so far!

Lem shot Skiff an annoyed look, and he tossed away the burned slide. "Listen up!" he shouted to the crowd. "We're not getting eaten or harvested or having our brains barbecued! The universe isn't scary." Lem paused, then lowering his voice, he added, "It's really . . . amazing."

For a second, the audience quieted. There was so much passion in Lem's voice that they believed what he was saying.

Lem focused on the dangling planets in the model space mobile. He yanked down a palm-sized planet and quickly wrapped its string around it. With a flick of his wrist, he used the planet like a yo-yo.

"Hey, kids!" he shouted. "Don't forget to pick up your planetary yo-yos!" He flicked the yo-yo again, and all the kids got quiet, staring at the toy. "We've got one for each of you," Lem finished.

Everyone in the crowd smiled and started to clap. Eckle jumped in front of Lem to be first in line to get a yo-yo.

Behind Lem, the curator smiled and made a big check mark on his clipboard.

Chapter 2

While kids filed out of the observatory, playing with their yo-yos, Eckle and Skiff stood outside the exit, waiting for Lem.

Finally, Lem burst through the doors with a big smile on his face. "You're looking at the new junior assistant curator!" he said cheerfully. He raised his hand for Skiff to slap. "High four!"

"High four!" Skiff repeated, slapping his four-fingered hand against Lem's.

The three friends walked down the hill back toward Main Street. They passed round houses along the base of the hill, groups of little stores, and the bushy park in the center of town.

"The job's part-time now, full-time after I

graduate," Lem explained. "I can see my whole life! A house. Two kids. Then *they'll* grow up and have kids. They'll come home to visit on holidays—" He pumped his fist in the air in excitement.

The mailman slowed his hovering mail truck near the boys. "Well?" the mailman asked Lem.

"I got it!" Lem replied happily.

After the mailman had pulled away, a police car floated up. Inside the patrol car's glass bubble, the officer raised his microphone to his lips. "Lem, congratulations on that job!" Chief Gorloc boomed through his car loudspeaker. "I expect big things from you!"

Lem gave the cop a thumbs-up. "Thanks, Chief!"

The three boys crossed the street to the movie theater. They peered up at the marquee, which had been changed during the afternoon, after Eckle had been ejected from the theater by his mother. The marquee now read: COMING SOON: *HUMANIACS III*! Near the front door, a huge poster for the movie showed a dramatic scene of aliens invading the planet. A banner over the poster announced: SIGN UP FOR THE PREMIERE COSTUME CONTEST!

"There it is," Skiff said breathlessly. "Only two more days."

With a cheer, Eckle spun around in place. *"Humaniacs III!"* he bellowed in a voice that was supposed to sound like a movie trailer announcer's. "The final battle for our world! Victory . . ."

Skiff joined in. "Or extinction!"

Lem stared at the banner for the costume contest. "If you guys go in costume," he warned, "I'm pretending we never met." He turned and strode down the street, away from the theater. "I'm a planetarium professional now. I don't have time for kids' movies anymore."

Skiff and Eckle both shook their heads, then ran after Lem.

"Kids' movies?" Skiff called. "Next you'll say aliens don't exist!"

Lem didn't reply. He just stopped walking and rolled his eyes.

"Just as I thought!" Skiff said, poking his finger

at Lem. "You're not Lem! You're an alien zombie like in *Humaniacs II*!"

"Skiff"—Lem sighed—"I'm not a zombie."

"Yeah, that's what you zombies are programmed to say," Skiff replied. He peered into Lem's face suspiciously. "Tell me something that the real Lem would know."

Lem smirked. "Well, I know Skiff is the only nutcase who thinks the government is hiding all alien evidence in Base 9."

Crossing his arms over his chest, Skiff still looked unconvinced.

"And," Lem continued, "you gave candy to your puppy so that he pooped jelly beans."

Eckle raised his eyebrows at Skiff.

Skiff nodded at Lem, sure now that he wasn't a zombie. Then Skiff noticed Eckle's surprised expression. "It was just an experiment!" he told the younger boy, then returned his attention to Lem. "With all due respect, I've done a lot of alien research at work."

Lem laughed. "What are you talking about?

You work in there!" He pointed at the store, Haglog Comics, that was right next to them. The store's bubble window was filled with colorful comic books, most of which had illustrations of alien invasions on their covers. The big sign on the roof had a model of a one-eyed alien in a space suit threatening the sidewalk with outstretched arms.

Skiff raised his chin. "Comic books are the greatest source of scientific knowledge."

"Skiff!" a voice hollered from inside the store. "Time to unpack the fake alien poop!" It was Skiff's boss.

"Right away, Mr. Hucklo!" Skiff called back.

Before he went inside, Skiff fixed Lem with a serious look. "You'll believe me when aliens put you on the take-out menu." He handed Eckle the latest *Humaniacs* comic book, which the younger boy took eagerly.

Then, as Skiff entered the store, he smiled and muttered, "I love fake alien poop day."

Eckle and Lem walked out of town, toward the suburban development where they both lived.

Although the houses were large and neatly kept, none of them had square corners, which made them look a bit like mushrooms. They all had bubble windows and domes for roofs, and were surrounded by pretty gardens and neat green lawns.

Lem stopped on their block, and ran his hand through his thick, squishy hair. "So . . . ," he began, sounding nervous, "um . . . Eckle . . . do you think your sister's home? I thought maybe . . . I might tell her I got the job."

"Why?" Eckle asked, kicking a rock on the sidewalk.

"Forget it," Lem said quickly. He lowered his eyes. "You tell her for me, okay?"

"Okay," Eckle agreed, booting the rock into the gutter. "But every time you tell me to tell her something, she asks why you don't just tell her yourself? And then my mom says it's because you like her, and then my sister says that's so cute and why don't you just ask her out already because she's been waiting for you to ask her out ever since we moved next door to you."

Lem blinked at the younger boy, his mouth dropping open. A hot blush rose in his cheeks. "She . . . has?" he asked. He broke out in a big grin. "The girl of my dreams likes me? This is the best day of my life!"

Eckle nodded. "And we got to see that kid throw up!"

Lem and Eckle walked up their driveways and headed into their connected backyards.

Behind Eckle's house, his father was busy lighting the barbecue while wearing a pink apron and humming a cheerful tune. Eckle's mother snapped a tablecloth in the air, letting it settle over the patio table. Neera, Eckle's sister, was on her knees beside the small garden on the far end of the yard, pulling out weeds.

Before Eckle could take a seat at the table, Lem's parents let out a cheer from their side of the lawn.

"He did it!" Lem's father shouted. He was wearing a nerdy red bow tie and red glasses. "Lem got the job!"

Smiling happily, Eckle's mother and father crossed

the lawn to congratulate Lem, who was being hugged by his parents.

"We're so proud of him!" Lem's mother gushed. She had pretty orange hair and was carrying a basket of roses.

As the two sets of parents chatted, Lem slipped away, and headed across the grass toward Neera.

Lem smiled nervously as he got closer to Eckle's sister. He could hear a romantic song playing in his head.

Hearing his footsteps, Neera got up on her feet, holding a tangle of limp weeds. She used her empty hand to brush grass off her purple skirt. Neera shifted her weight awkwardly from one foot to the other as Lem got closer, but she returned his smile.

"Hey, Neera," Lem said, "I wanted to tell you . . . I got the job."

Neera dropped her handful of weeds and clapped. "Lem, that's great!" she said. Overcome with excitement, Neera hugged him and gave him a quick kiss on the cheek.

Their faces flushed deeply, and they both took one awkward step backward.

"Uh . . . ," Lem mumbled, his cheek hot where she'd kissed him. "Um . . . now that I have a stable and rewarding career . . . ," he said, his voice cracking. "You know . . . I've been thinking—"

"Yes?" Neera prompted.

Lem smoothed down the front of his red and white shirt. "Um . . . maybe it's time that you and me—"

"Yes?" Neera repeated.

"I-I mean . . . ," Lem stammered, "would you want to—"

Before Lem could finish his question, he was interrupted by a battered, hippie-dippy car that came hovering down the driveway before clattering to a halt. Goofy, trippy music blared from the car's radio. Lem groaned when the car door popped open and Glar hopped out with his guitar.

Glar was the same age and Lem and Neera— sixteen—but he looked like he was from another planet, with his slouchy posture; funky clothes decorated with flowers and beads; and long, tangled yellow hair. He smiled at Neera and flashed her a peace sign. "I've been looking all over for you," he said to her in his low, mellow voice. "The cause needs you."

"The what?" Lem asked. He was irritated at being interrupted, and didn't like the way Neera was looking at Glar at all.

"The cause," Neera explained, sounding impressed. "Glar is involved in something he calls *protesting*. It's when you shout about something that makes you upset."

"Yeah!" Glar agreed. "Like the school pictures. Why do they have to be of our faces? I mean, what a bummer! That means *it's not good*." He smiled at Neera. "We need you, righteous mama!"

"I'm so honored, but . . . ," Neera began. She glanced back at Lem. "Lem was about to ask me something."

"What'd you want to ask her?" Glar asked,

leaning close to Lem.

Lem blinked, blushing faintly. "It's kind of private."

"No problemo, man," Glar said. "I totally respect that."

Lem faced Neera, taking a deep breath. "So—"

He was interrupted by Glar bursting out in song. "*Lem and Neera are having a private conversation,*" he crooned, strumming a folk tune on his guitar. "*Don't want anyone else around, so I'll keep out of their way . . . yeah!*"

Lem shook his head. "Yeah," he said flatly, "we can talk later."

Neera's shoulders slumped. "Okay," she said, and sighed. She strode over to Glar's side, and they headed toward his car.

Before he climbed in, Glar flashed a two-fingered sign to Lem. "Peace," he said. "That means *see ya later.*"

As Glar backed the car out of the driveway, Neera met Lem's eyes through the bubble's window. She bit her lip and quickly lowered her eyes.

Lem watched until the car took off down the street, and then let out a miserable sigh. He trudged into his house and headed up to his bedroom in the attic, which was a dark, domed space filled with science experiments; rounded, soft furniture; an oval TV; and a big telescope.

As soon as the door shut behind him, Lem hurried over to the telescope. He aimed it out his window down the block. Peering through the lens, Lem could just make out Glar's car disappearing into the distance.

Lem straightened up, his expression rueful and annoyed. "'The *cause*,'" he imitated Glar. "I'd like to cause him some pain!" He smacked the end of his telescope, which swiveled around and bashed the side of his head.

"Ow!" Lem grumbled. He smacked the telescope again, and it swung back toward the window, pointing up at the sky.

The telescope focused on a mysterious, fiery trail zooming down through the atmosphere.

Chapter 3

Sitting at his family's outdoor table, Eckle flipped through his comic book. He settled on a page featuring an alien attacking a small town, blasting down the houses with a laser that shot out of its single eye. "'Resistance is futile!'" Eckle read aloud. "'Surrender or die! Don't look at his eye!'"

Eckle's mother snatched the comic out of his hands. She tapped his head with it affectionately, and then pointed the book toward where Eckle's father was starting up the barbecue grill. "Come on," Eckle's mother said, "go help your father!"

As Eckle hopped off the bench, a strange rumbling filled the air and shook the ground. He peered around but didn't see anything unusual except for his parents and Lem's parents in the yard next door all glancing around nervously, too. Then Eckle looked up.

The clouds above their houses were churning with reddish smoke. Eckle's mouth dropped open when a silver spaceship descended through the clouds. The ship fired its central retrorocket, slowing as it lowered toward the ground.

The spaceship was small—more of a landing module than a long-distance starship. It was bizarrely angular, with lots of weird square edges glinting in the sunlight.

As Eckle watched, his heart pounding, the ship extended four narrow legs out of its sides. Then, with a last blast of its retrorocket, it settled down on Eckle's family's lawn.

People all around the neighborhood peered over fences and hedges, or gaped through open doorways and windows at the alien ship that had just landed. Nobody moved. Everyone was in shock.

The front hatch on the spaceship suddenly slid open. It made a depressurizing noise, like the slow opening of a bottle of fizzy soda.

And then an . . . an astronaut stepped out.

The astronaut was wearing a silver space suit and a mirrored bubble helmet. The alien leaped out of the hatch and jumped a few steps into the middle of the lawn, waving a long pole with a flag attached to it. The flag had red and white stripes, and a blue square in an upper corner decorated with white stars. He moved in slow motion for some reason, bouncing off the ground like he was pretending this planet had low gravity.

With great solemnity, the astronaut jammed the pole into the ground and then stepped back to admire the flapping flag.

Nobody in Eckle's neighborhood moved at all. The totally unexpected invasion had frozen everyone in place.

Then the astronaut looked around the area. He stiffened in his space suit—perhaps he'd been expecting an empty, desolate landscape instead of the cheerful, populated suburb in which he'd landed.

For a long moment, the townspeople and the astronaut stared silently at one another. Then Eckle grinned, pulled a pen out from behind his ear, and headed over to the astronaut to get his autograph.

As the astronaut and all the townspeople stared at him, Eckle crossed the lawn toward the spaceship. Close up, Eckle could see that the astronaut had another red, white, and blue flag patch on his shoulder, and a badge on the front of his space suit that read NASA.

The astronaut took a nervous step backward when Eckle raised his comic book and pen. At the same time, the automatic lawn sprinkler behind the astronaut whizzed up between him and his spaceship. Then Lem's father accidentally squeezed lighter fluid onto his barbecue grill, and a jet of flame shot into the air.

Panicking, the astronaut whirled around and ran off down the street. Lem opened his house's front door just in time to see the astronaut sprinting toward town.

Everyone gathered in the street to watch as the astronaut got freaked out by a barking dog and stepped onto a boy's antigravity skateboard. The skateboard sent the astronaut zooming, his arms whirling wildly, into the center of town, where cars screeched to a halt to avoid running him over.

Finally, the astronaut slammed against a car's windshield. The driver of the car opened his door and ran away screaming, and the astronaut ran off in the other direction. He bolted toward the hills on the edge of town, disappearing into the woods below the observatory.

The next morning, while Lem was getting ready to go to school, he stopped to watch the TV in his family's living room. A popular anchorman was reporting the news of the alien invasion in a worried voice. "Are the aliens hostile?" the anchorman intoned. "Will our species survive? One thing we do know is that they show no respect for our parking laws."

Lem gathered a pile of his schoolbooks and headed out the front door. The sight of the spaceship on the neighbor's lawn stopped him in his tracks. Even though nobody had been able to talk about anything else since the landing, it was still hard to believe that an alien spacecraft was right there in front of him. He shook his head at the police officers trying to keep curious people from getting too close, and set off toward school.

Inside the school, Lem stopped to peek into a classroom of younger kids, where the female teacher in front of the class was holding a pamphlet entitled *So You've Been Invaded by Aliens*.

"All right, class," the teacher said. "Let's try it one more time. . . ."

Lem jumped in surprise when the teacher screamed "Aliens are coming!"

All the students dived under their desks, taking cover.

One chunky boy became confused and didn't make it under his desk. "Flarc," the teacher called, "you were too slow. Go join the zombies."

With a sigh, Flarc trudged to the back of the classroom. He joined a group of sad-looking kids in a roped-off corner. On the rope was a sign that read ZOMBIES.

Lem shook his head. Yesterday had been a deeply strange day, and he had a feeling today was only going to get weirder.

After the final bell of the day rang, Lem met up with Skiff in front of the school. Skiff was lounging on the school's steps, and Lem paced nervously around him.

"Did I call it or did I call it?" Skiff asked proudly. "The only question is, should I be terrified because it's the end of the world, or happy because I totally called it? Me, I have a plan. They're going to need a native to run the mines. I'll befriend them, show my executive skills, and *bam*, I'm in!"

Lem rolled his eyes. "I've got to get to work," he said.

A little while later, Lem stood in front of his open locker in the employee break room in the planetarium, thinking about Neera. "Neera, you have to choose," he said firmly. "It's either me or Glar!"

Lem wiggled the locker door, which made the picture of Neera that he'd taped up inside the door wiggle, too. She almost looked as though she were talking. "Oh, Lem!" he said in a high-pitched voice. "There's no question . . . it's you, of course!"

Lem smiled and closed the locker.

After working in the planetarium all afternoon with no major disasters, Lem headed back through the observatory toward the break room. He was alone in the building now—the curator had trusted him to close down the museum for the evening.

The main room of the observatory was a huge circular chamber filled with scientific space exhibits and big dioramas of the universe. In the middle of the room there were giant telescopes and rotating globes; and under the high, round dome, there were enormous hanging mobiles of planets and stars. Lem found the control panel and began switching off the lights.

Lem didn't notice that the alien astronaut was sleeping, hidden in one of the display dioramas behind a ringed planet.

A red light on the astronaut's chest suddenly started blinking and buzzing, waking him up. He struggled to pull himself into a sitting position. "Huh," he muttered. "It looks like Rover's been activated." Then he stretched his legs, knocking two of the rings off the model planet. They clattered to the floor.

Nearby, Lem heard the racket. He stepped toward the diorama display, curious about what had made the noise.

He reached the display just as the astronaut climbed to his feet.

Lem and the astronaut stood face-to-helmet. In the mirrored surface, Lem could see his own startled reflection.

At the exact same moment, both Lem and the astronaut screamed and ran away in opposite directions.

Chapter 4

Lem, screaming, ran to the right along the wall. The astronaut, also screaming—although his cries were muffled inside his helmet—ran to the left, keeping tight to the wall as well. In their panicked scramble to escape each other, Lem knocked over a display of meteors, while the astronaut bashed an EXIT sign and whacked into the ticket counter, toppling the flimsy booth.

Since they both were keeping to the wall as they rushed away, and the room was circular, and they were both fleeing in opposite directions . . . they collided on the other side of the domed chamber—headlong and hard.

Smash!

They both fell back on their butts. Then, shaking off the surprise, they sat up straight and screamed again. Lem hopped to his feet, heading for the telephone in the ticket booth.

The astronaut took longer to get up because of his bulky suit. His helmet was knocked askew. Blindly, he bolted toward the middle of the room and tried to dive into the safety of an information kiosk. But midleap he hit the low wires of a big, hanging planetary mobile. The astronaut struggled against the cords and got hopelessly tangled up, dangling in space a few feet off the ground.

When Lem reached the overturned ticket booth, he checked behind him and was surprised that the alien wasn't chasing him. When he saw that the alien was all tangled up, he stopped to watch the strange sight of an astronaut squirming in the air like he was floating in zero gravity.

The astronaut lurched suddenly, flipping himself over. The hose connecting his air supply to his helmet got snagged on a wire and popped loose.

The room filled with the hissing sound of escaping air.

Realizing he was in trouble, the astronaut stiffened. Then he bent himself double to check the air gauge on the front of his space suit. The digital numbers were quickly lowering. He screamed again in panic and squirmed.

Lem backed up toward the fallen ticket booth, and kneeled to retrieve the phone from the wreckage. He sighed with relief when he saw that the phone wasn't damaged and still had a dial tone. He quickly pushed buttons on the front panel. "C'mon," he muttered impatiently.

"Hello!" a cheerful voice answered. "This is the alien hotline."

"Yes, hi," Lem said quickly. "I found the alien—"

"They're here," the voice chirped, "and no weapon can stop them! Please hold."

Lem groaned. "You've got to be kidding." A happy tune played while he waited impatiently.

Meanwhile, the numbers on the astronaut's air

gauge sunk until the digital readout flashed the word EMPTY. He sagged against the wires, twitching and choking out gasps, letting his arms fall limp.

The on-hold music continued chiming in Lem's ear.

Lem grimaced sympathetically as the wires supporting the astronaut suddenly snapped, dropping him to the floor with a loud *thud*.

The astronaut lay still.

Lem watched him carefully. The alien didn't move at all. He was probably dead.

Biting his lip, Lem pressed the phone tighter against his ear, and took two careful steps toward the unmoving astronaut.

The astronaut suddenly jumped to his feet. He waved his arms frantically, gagging and choking, weaving unsteadily. Finally, he straightened up and grabbed his helmet with his gloved hands. He snapped the lock loose and twisted the helmet to the side.

Then the alien pulled the helmet off.

Lem gasped when he saw the strange creature's face.

He looked to be in his mid-thirties, with a long, rectangular head and a strong jaw. His hair was blondish red and cropped short. He had no antennae at all, and his nose stuck out from his face, with tiny holes in its base. Yes, he looked strange, but . . . not all that different from Lem, even though the alien's skin was pinkish instead of green. In fact, Lem had a feeling that on his own planet, the alien astronaut was considered handsome.

The astronaut's face grew redder and his cheeks puffed out—he was holding his breath. But he couldn't keep it up for more than a few moments, and finally he let out a frightened breath, and then inhaled deeply, his eyes terrified.

To the astronaut's surprise, the air was fine. He took another deep breath, more confidently.

"I can breathe!" The alien gasped out in amazement.

Lem took another step toward the astronaut, but was pulled up short by the phone cord. "You speak my language," he said.

"That's amazing!" the alien said in a deep, firm

voice, like an announcer on television . . . or a superhero. "You speak my language."

"That's what I just said," Lem pointed out.

The astronaut smiled. "You just said, 'That's what I just said,'" he said. "Say something else!"

Lem scratched the side of his squishy hair. "Like what?"

"'Like . . . what!'" the alien repeated, pleased by his ability to understand. "They're going to freak back at Kennedy!"

Lem didn't understand what a "Kennedy" might be, and he remembered that he was dealing with a strange alien creature . . . who was standing between himself and the exit. He tightened his grip on the phone.

The alien pressed his gloved hand against his chest. "I'm Captain Charles T. Baker," he introduced himself. "Better known as Chuck. I'm an astronaut. As . . . tro . . . naut."

"Ass—," Lem began.

"Tronaut!" the alien finished triumphantly.

Lem pointed at himself repeatedly. "Lem . . . Lem . . . Lem . . ."

Chuck tilted his head quizzically at Lem, as though trying to understand something difficult. "I believe . . . ," he said, "your name . . . is Lem."

Rolling his eyes at the slowness of Chuck's uptake, Lem asked, "What do you want?" His voice still sounded pretty nervous.

"Thanks for asking," Chuck said, tucking his helmet under his arm. "Coffee light, two sugars. A frappuccino would be even better, along with any puff pastry—"

"I mean . . . ," Lem interrupted, "are you here to take over our world, and . . . eat our brains?" He couldn't help gulping in fear.

Chuck blinked at him, and then screwed up his face in disgust. "Whoa, hold on!" he cried. "What kind of sick planet *is* this? First of all, it's supposed to be uninhabited, okay? Not full of sea monkeys dancing to the oldies! My mission was to plant Old Glory, whack a few golf balls, and head on back for the Kids' Choice Awards. I'm getting slimed. . . ." Chuck let his words trail off when he saw the bewildered expression on Lem's face. "What?" he asked.

"You were just talking alien," Lem replied.

"Hey," Chuck said, squinting his eyes. "I'm not the alien here . . . you are."

"Me?" Lem squealed. "*You* are."

Chuck shook his head. "No, you are."

"You are," Lem said firmly. "You came to *my* planet."

Chuck laughed. "An *alien* planet!" Then he took a moment to catch his breath. "Let's start over," he said in a calm voice. "Look . . . there's a command module in orbit right now, running out of fuel. It has to leave in"—he looked down at the digital readout on his chest—"seventy-four hours. And if I'm not on it, it goes back to Earth without me. Got it?"

After thinking about Chuck's words, Lem shook his head in befuddlement.

"I have to get to my ship and go back up in

space," Chuck said simply. "Can you help me?"

Lem's eyes widened. "You want me to take you to your flying saucer? If they catch me helping you, who knows what they'd do to me! I'll lose everything! And my life was just getting perfect."

"Kid . . . ," Chuck said, scratching his chin. "You're a kid, right? You're not like a thousand-year-old Yoda?" When Lem just stared blankly, the astronaut continued. "Never mind. Kid, you're my only hope. But . . . I suppose you could leave me stranded. My wife will have to support the kids. *Eleven* kids. Always hungry. But hey, they'll get by without a father. The important thing is, you avoid a little trouble."

Lem looked down at the floor. Chuck's guilt trip was hitting home. Then the phone in his hand squawked.

"Alien hotline!" a female voice chirped. "What's the nature of your sighting?"

Lem was completely unsure about what he should do.

"Hello, are you there?" the woman prompted. "Alien hotline!"

Lem stared at the phone. Then he glanced up at Chuck, who made a begging motion with his hands, his expression desperately pleading.

Lem heaved a big sigh, and made the decision that would change his life.

Lem puttered into the suburbs in his old red and white car, with Chuck hiding in the backseat. The car didn't have a glass bubble like the newer models—it had only a round blue canopy on top to keep out the rocky rain. It wasn't the fanciest ride, and it looked more like a golf cart than a car, but Lem was proud of it. It had taken him ages to save up enough to buy it.

He slowed down as he got closer to his family's house. There was still a crowd gathered near the spaceship, with onlookers standing behind cordons of yellow police tape. The anchorman whom Lem had seen on TV that morning was standing by his station's trailer, getting his makeup applied while taking notes on a script. Scanning the surroundings, Lem spotted at least six police officers overseeing the area, including Chief Gorloc.

Lem stopped in front of his driveway. "There's your flying saucer," he whispered back to Chuck. "What now?"

Chuck peeped over the edge of the car, glancing around at the busy scene. He set his strong jaw firmly. "Okay, here's the plan," he decided. "You knock out that cop." He pointed to a skinny officer chatting with two young women. "Then you overpower those two." Chuck nodded to indicate two cops having coffee by their hovering squad cars, and then he pointed at Chief Gorloc and his portly deputy. "You neutralize that one, and handcuff the big guy to the steering wheel."

"That's your plan?" Lem hissed. "What if they start *shooting*?"

Chuck shrugged, his space suit crinkling. "You're one of their own—they'll probably aim for your legs. Don't your legs grow back?"

"No," Lem replied, shaking his head. "We're not like your kind."

After thinking for a moment, Chuck pulled a chocolate bar out of a pouch on his suit. "Tell you what . . . eat this," he suggested. "You become invincible."

"Oh, good!" Lem said sarcastically, rolling his eyes and pushing away the chocolate bar. "Then you do it!"

Chuck inhaled sharply as though offended. "I can't be seen breaking the law," he explained. "I've got the Right Stuff."

"The *what*?" Lem asked.

"The Right Stuff," the astronaut repeated. "That means I have a lot of courage." He suddenly ducked into the backseat, hiding from a little girl who had wandered too close. "Now go," he ordered.

Lem didn't move. It didn't sound like a good plan at all, but it wasn't like he had a plan of his own.

While Lem was hesitating, Chuck reached around and popped Lem's door open. Then he shoved Lem roughly out of the car.

"Go on!" Chuck commanded. "Go, go, go!"

Chapter 5

Lem stumbled toward the officers, who had their backs to him. He managed to regain his balance before he slammed into the cops. Standing right behind them, Lem glanced back at the car, where Chuck was peering over the edge of the door.

Chuck sliced his hand downward, gesturing for Lem to attack with a judo chop.

That seemed like such a bad idea. Shaking his head, Lem stepped backward and bumped into one of the policemen. Lem whirled around and came face-to-face with Chief Gorloc.

"Oh, hi, Lem," the chief said pleasantly. "Something wrong?"

Lem snuck a peek back at his car. He smiled at

Chief Gorloc uneasily. "Uh, well—"

A commotion from down the street made everyone turn to look. An army battalion was barreling toward them. Hovering green jeeps, huge round tanks, trucks, and domed transporters filled with soldiers pulled up to a stop on the suburban street.

Soldiers in their brown uniforms teemed out of the trucks and transporters. Their antennae wiggled as they raced to line up in formation and surround the spaceship.

Lem shot a glance at his own car, and saw that Chuck had ducked down far enough to be completely hidden. Then Lem had to jump out of the way as a TV reporter and his news crew pushed past him to film the action.

A Humvee arrived in an empty spot, and the soldiers turned toward it. A fat army captain with a squishy green mustache stepped in front of the crowd. "Attention!" he shouted, and all the soldiers stood up straight, on high alert.

A tall, muscular general climbed calmly out of the Humvee. His brown uniform was sharp and crisp, and decorated with three stars and two medals. The general was wearing dark sunglasses, and his crew cut was perfect and neat, with long antennae sticking out of it.

He paced in front of the soldiers, his walk haughty with authority. "So," the general said, staring up at the spaceship. "They've come." He strode over to where the fat captain was standing near the spaceship. "Captain, have your men search the flying saucer," he ordered.

The captain saluted. "Yes, General Grawl, sir!" He beckoned with his hand toward one of the covered trucks. Immediately, a group of soldiers wearing bulky radiation suits marched down the truck's ramp and bustled over to the spaceship. They filed in through the ship's hatch. Another squad of soldiers held their rifles ready in case the soldiers in radiation suits met any resistance.

Lem spotted Chuck's head peeping over the edge of his car door. The astronaut was frowning, obviously unhappy that his spaceship was being searched. Backing up slowly, Lem tried to make his way toward his car, but there were too many soldiers around him. He stopped and forced a smile to show the soldiers that he was harmless.

One soldier in a radiation suit stuck his head back out of the hatch. "No sign of the pilot, sir!" he reported.

A minute later, the soldiers began to exit the spaceship, carrying objects they'd found inside. Their arms were overflowing with magazines, packets of astronaut food and ice cream, bottles of hair products, and unidentifiable gadgets.

As the soldiers were carrying the objects back to the truck, one of them stumbled on a curb. An MP3 player slid off the top of his pile and landed in the street. It clicked on, and music started blaring from its headphones.

Screaming, the soldiers ran and ducked, covering their ears.

Three gunshots rang out. The MP3 player shattered and the music ceased.

Everyone looked up at General Grawl, who had fired the shots. He put away his gun and nodded grimly. "I have never seen such a heinous weapon," he growled. "We are up against a cruel, sadistic enemy." He turned slowly, waving his arm at the troops. "Seal off the town!" he ordered. "I want that alien pilot found!"

"I protest!" yelled a voice from the crowd of onlookers.

Lem rolled his eyes when he saw Glar step onto the lawn, holding up his guitar. Right behind him were a bunch of his teenage followers . . . and Neera.

Glar strummed his guitar loudly. "Daddy-o," he told General Grawl, "you're bumming me out with those bad vibrations!"

The general blinked at Glar, taking in his long, yellow hair and hippie clothing. "Never mind, Captain," Grawl said. "The alien's right here."

"Grab him!" the captain commanded.

Two soldiers rushed over and grabbed Glar's arms, pinning them behind him. His guitar fell to the grass.

Neera sprang in front of Glar, her eyes furious. "Glar's not the alien!"

"Oh, no?" General Grawl shot back. He grabbed a hunk of Glar's long, yellow hair. "Then what do you call *this*?"

"Hair!" Neera replied. She forced herself to take a deep breath so that she wouldn't get too angry. "He likes it long."

The general raised his bushy eyebrows. "Very unusual," he said, letting go of Glar's hair and wiping his hands on his jacket. "You might even say . . . *very alien*!"

A teacher from Lem's school stepped out from the crowd of townspeople. She adjusted her big round glasses and cleared her throat. "Excuse me, General," the teacher said. "Glar does go to the local high school."

General Grawl let his shoulders relax a little, and he turned away from Glar.

"Glar's just trying to say the aliens might be friendly," Neera explained. Then she spotted Lem, who was inching backward toward his car. "Lem!" she called.

Lem froze in place, smiling worriedly.

"Lem, you know astronomy," Neera said. Her expression was begging him to help her out. "If an alien came all this way . . . wouldn't it be smart enough to come in peace?"

For a second Lem felt thrilled that she had asked him for help. But before he could answer, he saw that a soldier was peering into his car. The soldier reached for the door handle—

"No!" Lem hollered. He pushed Neera harshly aside and rushed over to his car, jumping between the soldier and the door, blocking him from opening it.

Leaning against the car door, Lem realized that everybody was staring at him. A shadow of suspicion crossed the general's face.

"Um . . . I mean . . . ," Lem began, trying to cover for his behavior. "They've come to harvest our organs! Make us slaves! We should all go home and hide!"

General Grawl nodded. "Now that's a sensible young man." He waved the soldiers away from the car. "Let him go." Then the general addressed the throng of townspeople. "And the rest of you!" he called out. "Go to your homes and wait for instructions!"

Before the general changed his mind, Lem hopped into his car and started it up. The crowd had begun dispersing as soon as the general told them to, so Lem was able to pull into his driveway. The soldiers guarding the entrance backed up as Lem eased the car toward his house.

Lem gulped when he saw Neera pulling herself up off her knees after he'd pushed her and she'd fallen. He winced when he saw the hurt, angry expression on her face . . . she was obviously disgusted by his refusal to help her.

Then Glar put his arm around Neera's shoulder, helping her up, and Lem got so worked up that he almost drove off the asphalt and onto the lawn. He forced himself to remain calm. He couldn't do anything about the situation with an alien astronaut in his backseat and soldiers surrounding the house.

Clutching the steering wheel tightly, Lem drove his car into the garage and closed the door.

Lem quickly ushered Chuck into the house and snuck him up to his bedroom. He shut the door behind them and pulled down all the window shades.

With his hands tightened into fists, Chuck stood stiffly in the middle of Lem's bedroom, steaming with frustration. "Great!" he complained. "Just great!"

Lem let out an annoyed grunt and headed over to the window. "Look," he told Chuck, "I said I'd take you to your flying saucer. Well, there it is!" He pulled open the window shade, revealing the spaceship on the lawn. "Now leave!"

Identical expressions of shock crossed Lem's and Chuck's faces as more military troops marched into view. They formed a circle three-deep around the ship, while another group of soldiers set up big artillery guns nearby. A truck in the driveway aimed a giant spotlight at the spaceship and flooded it with bright light.

There was no way to sneak Chuck past all those soldiers into the ship, especially with it illuminated as bright as day. Lem pulled down the shade, feeling totally discouraged.

Lem headed toward the door. "I'll get you a

blanket and pillow for the night."

Chuck shifted a corner of the window shade and peeked out. "It's a miracle I'm going to need."

Later that night, Lem set up a sleeping bag on the floor for Chuck. Chuck was dressed in a pair of Lem's father's pajamas and eating a candy bar. He raised the remote control and flicked on the TV.

When Lem came out of the bathroom in his pajamas, he heard the TV announcer intone, "When aliens invade!" The picture switched to an image of a scientist standing in front of a blackboard. The scientist was old and tiny, with a huge head and long, skinny antennae. He was wearing a white lab coat, black gloves, and a giant monocle. On his head was a beanie with a small metal dish attached to it.

"Professor Kipple," the announcer stated in voice-over, "you are the foremost authority on aliens. What can you tell us so we know how to be prepared?"

Professor Kipple nodded his huge head. "Aliens are quite like us," he answered in a calm, reassuring voice. "Except they have two sets of teeth, hypodermic fingertips, and hypnotic eyes to control our brains . . . and turn us into zombies and destroy our world."

"*What . . . ?*" Chuck protested.

The tiny professor raised a finger and shook it. "Remember, anyone caught helping the aliens will go to jail."

Lem grabbed the remote and clicked off the TV. He climbed under the covers, unable to remember ever feeling so tired in his life. After turning off the light, Lem stared up at the ceiling. "*Jail,*" he said flatly. "Yesterday my life was perfect. Now I'm the most wanted criminal in the world."

Chuck settled into his sleeping bag. "At least you have a world," he replied in a whisper. He stared up at the ceiling, too. "I'll probably never see mine again."

Chapter 6

In the morning, both Lem and Chuck sat up straight in their beds when a loud knock on Lem's bedroom door woke them up.

The door started to swing open. Lem jumped out of bed and stumbled to the door to block it. "Mom, don't come in!" he gasped.

He tried to push the door closed, but it wouldn't shut all the way. Lem glanced down and saw a chunky rubber tire with deep treads wedged against the door. He blinked, confused. Lem eased the door open to get a better look.

There in the hallway was a small alien robot. He was white and shaped like a rectangular box, with six off-road ready tires, a solar panel on his back, a long communications antenna, and a globe-shaped white head. On his head was a wide, round camera lens, which whirred as it focused on Lem's face.

Lem backed away from the robot, terrified by the invader.

The robot chirped once and zipped past Lem, beeping as he rolled toward Chuck. When he reached the astronaut's space suit on a chair near Chuck, he stopped short and beeped rapidly. The red light on Chuck's suit blinked in sync with the red light on the robot's control panel.

"Rover?" Chuck asked happily. "Boy, am I glad to see you!" Chuck got up on his knees and inched toward the robot. He patted him on the head like a dog. "Rover!"

"Rover?" Lem repeated, feeling bewildered. It was too early in the morning for visits from alien robots. He shut the door.

Chuck laughed as Rover nuzzled his hand with his pivoting head. "He's a robot probe we sent to take pictures of your world," Chuck explained. After thinking about what he'd just said, Chuck wagged his finger, scolding the robot. "A planet full of aliens," he said grumpily, "and you send back hundreds of pictures of *rocks*? Bad boy!"

Rover let his head droop and let out a sad whine.

Happy to have company from Earth, even if it was only a robot, Chuck pulled on his space suit.

There was another knock on the door. Lem rushed over to it. "Mom, don't come in!" But he was too late again.

Eckle stood in the open doorway. The young boy's eyes lit up when he saw an astronaut kneeling on the sleeping bag next to a robot probe. "Wow!" Eckle yelped. "The alien!" He pulled a comic book out of his back pocket and held it out to the astronaut. "Can I get your autograph?"

Lem grabbed Eckle's arm and tried to push him out the doorway. "This isn't a comic book, okay?" he grumbled. "It's serious!"

"I don't mind," Chuck said. He stood up, grabbed a pen off Lem's desk, and strode over to the doorway. "It comes with being a national hero."

While Chuck was signing the comic book, Eckle pulled another item out of his pocket, and unfolded it.

"Sign my *Humaniacs* poster, too!" Eckle begged.

Chuck signed the poster.

Then Eckle lifted his shirt, showing his shiny green torso. "And sign my chest!"

Chuck hesitated, his pen outstretched. "Um . . . ," he said. Then he noticed a camera sitting on Lem's desk shelf. "How about a snapshot, instead?" Chuck struck a heroic pose, as though staring dreamily up at space. "Get one of me looking up at the stars."

For the third time that morning, there was a knock at the door. Chuck and Lem exchanged a nervous look, and then Lem reached for the door. "Mom . . . !"

Before Lem could reach the door, it swung open.

Skiff sauntered in on his skinny legs, already talking. "Lem, I saw the alien last night! I am so in. I've got this guy wrapped around my little finger. Let me tell you, this alien is not so scary. . . ."

Skiff's words trailed off as he noticed the

astronaut and the probe in the bedroom. He twitched once, and then saluted Chuck, sharply standing at attention. "Your personal chef reporting for duty, sir!" he said. "May I give you some tasty suggestions for tonight? I have a list of the twenty fattest teachers in my school in case you're looking for a light snack—"

"Skiff, stop," Lem ordered. "He's not here to eat us or anything. He's harmless." Lem winced, remembering the disaster with Neera yesterday. "To everyone but me," he added.

Putting his hand on Lem's shoulder, Skiff shook his head sadly. "Better let me do the talking," he said. "I think he's eyeing you for dessert."

Then Skiff jumped a little when Rover whirred over beside him. The robot inspected Skiff with his eye, and then rubbed his head against Skiff's leg affectionately. It took a second for Skiff to relax, but when he saw Rover's adorable expression, blinking his camera eye and tilting his head, Skiff softened and patted the probe. "Aw," he muttered, "it's kind of cute the way he does that."

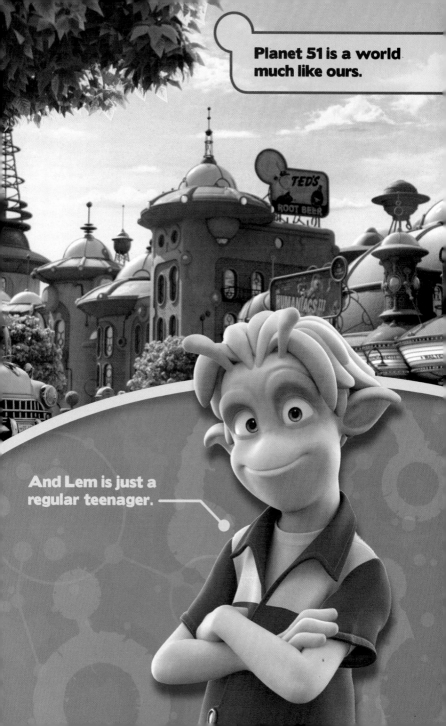

Planet 51 is a world much like ours.

And Lem is just a regular teenager.

He's enjoying a barbecue with his family when the sky suddenly turns gray.

A spaceship appears out of nowhere and lands in the yard!

Who is this strange creature from outer space?

It's Chuck Baker, astronaut and Earthling!

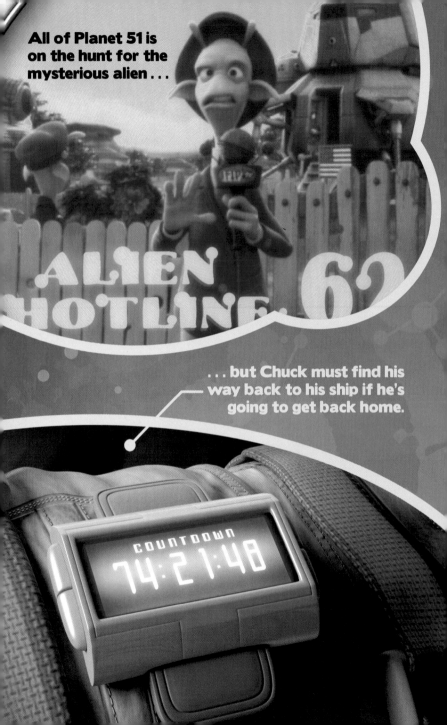

All of Planet 51 is on the hunt for the mysterious alien . . .

ALIEN HOTLINE 62

. . . but Chuck must find his way back to his ship if he's going to get back home.

COUNTDOWN
74:21:48

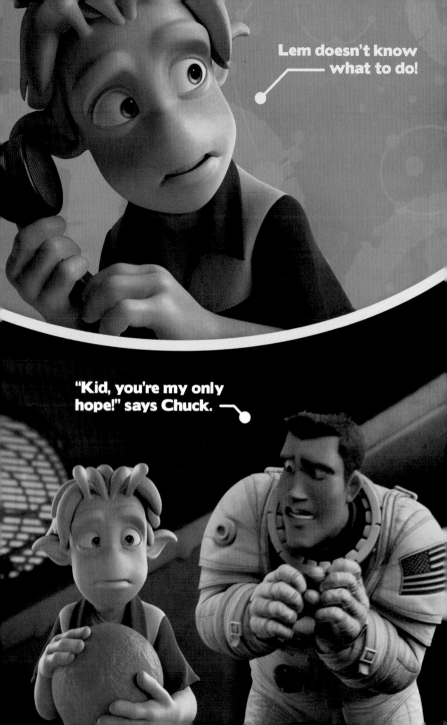

Rover, Chuck's robot, is ready to roll.

Luckily, Lem's friends Eckle and Skiff are also willing to help Chuck.

Eckle knows all about Chuck's alien habits.

Together, they help Chuck find his ship.

Rover nuzzled against Skiff, and Skiff kneeled down to tickle the robot under his chin. The probe let out a pleased whine.

Then there was another knock on the door. Lem groaned, and marched over to the door. "Great!" he complained. "Let's just have a party!" He opened the door a crack and peeked out.

Two soldiers in their brown uniforms stood in the hallway. One was solid and muscular; the other was short and skinny. Neither looked very bright.

"I'm Private Vesklin," the skinny soldier said. "This is Private Vernkot." He nodded toward the muscular soldier. "We're doing a routine search for the alien."

Before Lem could reply, the soldiers pushed past him into his bedroom.

When they saw Chuck and Rover, their mouths dropped open in shock. The soldiers fumbled awkwardly, raising their rifles and aiming at the aliens.

"Don't shoot!" Chuck screamed.

Private Vernkot squinted like he was in pain. "He's trying to control our minds!"

"What do we do?" Private Vesklin screeched.

Vernkot twisted his muscular body, turning his head away from Chuck. "Don't look at its eyes!" he cried. "That's how they take over your brain!"

Rubbing his chin, Chuck murmured, "Brains?" He realized he could use their confusion to his advantage. "*Braaaains . . . ,*" he moaned. "That's right! *Braaaains.* You are my zombie slaves! I want to control your brains. . . ." He wiggled his fingers and made a high-pitched sound like a science-fiction alien spaceship taking off.

"It's inside my head," Vesklin whimpered.

Gritting his teeth, Vernkot pressed his hands against the sides of his head. "His will is too strong!"

Lem and Eckle stared at the soldiers, amazed at how quickly they were brainwashed.

Vesklin dropped his arms along the sides of his skinny body, and stared at Chuck with empty eyes. "Command us, Master!" he said robotically.

"Command us, Master!" Vernkot agreed.

Skiff lurched in front of the soldiers. "Command me, too!"

Lem pulled Skiff toward him. "It's not real," he hissed in Skiff's ear.

Skiff raised his chin and pressed his fingers against his chest. "I think I know when I'm being mind-controlled," he said haughtily.

Stepping away from the soldiers, Chuck grabbed Lem's shoulder and steered him over to the window. "Hey," he whispered, "maybe they can get me on my ship."

Lifting a corner of the window shade, Lem peered down at the military operation surrounding the spaceship. He sighed. "Probably not . . . ," he admitted, but then he looked over at the TV, which Eckle had just flipped on. The anchorman was doing a report about the spaceship from the yard outside. "But I think I know who can."

Lem stiffened when he heard loud talking coming from downstairs. He put his finger to his lips, and sneaked out into the hall. Peering over the edge of the upstairs banister, he could see the front door, where his mother was talking to General Grawl and the captain in the open doorway. Lem's stomach lurched.

"General, how about some breakfast for you and your men?" Lem's mother offered. "You need your strength to fight that alien!"

Lem's father hurried down the hallway toward the front door, straightening his bow tie. "You want our home for your headquarters?" he suggested. "It would be a great honor." He turned to face his wife. "Honey, tell Lem we have guests."

Lem shrunk back against the hallway wall when his mother peered up. *"Le-em . . . ,"* she called up, "there's someone here you'd like to meet!"

"Be right down, Mom!" he replied.

Daring to peek over the banister again, Lem saw his parents leading the captain and the general into the kitchen.

Lem hurried back into his bedroom. "We've got to get out of here . . . now!" he told everyone. Then Lem led them all quickly and silently down the stairs and through a hall door into the garage. Chuck ordered Vesklin and Vernkot to go out and drive a jeep back into the garage. Still thinking they were brainwashed, the soldiers did as they were told.

When the jeep was safely in the garage, and the garage door closed, Chuck and Rover got in and hid under a blanket in the backseat, with Eckle, Skiff, and Lem sitting around them. Vesklin got in the driver's seat, and Vernkot took shotgun. Then Lem opened the garage door, and Vesklin pulled the jeep out into the driveway.

"Act normal," Chuck warned the soldiers, and they smiled cheerfully, waving to the other soldiers teeming all over the yard. Vesklin exited the driveway and backed up onto the street.

As they passed the TV truck, Lem nodded, getting an idea. "Head to the center of town," he instructed Vesklin. The rifle in the backseat kept bumping against Lem's arm, so he pulled it onto his lap where it was more comfortable.

Lem looked around Main Street as they passed the quiet stores. "All we need is a safe place and a TV reporter."

"So, wait . . . ," Chuck said, sticking his head out from under the blanket. "You think you can get me on TV?"

Lem nodded, shifting the rifle in his lap so that it poked up over his shoulder. "You're the biggest story in history," he replied. "The whole planet will watch."

Chuck smiled. "The whole planet?" he said. "Interesting." He peered into the reflection of his wristwatch, and smoothed down his hair. "I left my hair products on the ship, but I could improvise. Astronauts have to deal with any kind of emergency."

"I get it," Eckle said. "He can tell everyone he's peaceful!"

"Yep," Lem confirmed. "Then we can all get on with our lives." He glanced at Chuck, and shifted the rifle to his other shoulder. "With you out of mine."

Lem looked out the window as they were passing the park in the middle of town. Neera was standing by the gazebo, along with Glar and the group of teenage protesters. Lem smiled—Neera looked so pretty. "Hey, Neera!" he called out.

Neera started to return Lem's smile, but then her eyes squinted, and she frowned angrily. "Kill any aliens, Lem?" she asked in an icy voice.

For a second, Lem didn't understand what she was talking about. But then he remembered that he was sitting in a jeep with two soldiers . . . and holding a rifle over his shoulder. "No!" he protested. "You don't understand. These soldiers aren't . . ." Lem gave up, realizing there was no way he could explain. "Oh, great, this just gets better and better."

All he could do was shake his head miserably as Vesklin drove the jeep past the park, leaving Neera glaring at him, completely getting the wrong idea.

Chapter 7

The jeep pulled around the back of the comic book store, and Chuck ordered Vesklin to park behind some big garbage cans to hide the vehicle somewhat.

Skiff unlocked the back door, and everyone filed out of the jeep and into the store.

The cluttered, murky store was filled with racks of colorful comics, life-sized cardboard cutouts of science-fiction monsters and aliens, and shelves and displays of creature models and spaceship toys. The walls were lined with movie posters and ads for comics.

Eckle and the soldiers made a beeline for the comics, quickly pulling new issues from the racks.

Lem pulled down the window shades, then slumped down on a stool in the corner, burying his face in his hands. He couldn't believe how awful things had become with Neera. He couldn't remember the last time he'd managed to say the right thing to her.

Chuck noticed Lem looking miserable, sitting on the stool. He strode across the store over to him. "Kid, what's bugging you?"

Lem raised his head momentarily. "Neera."

Chuck snorted. "What is that, like an alien hernia?"

"Sort of," Lem replied, dangling his feet. "Neera is the girl of my dreams. Now she hates me."

"*Hate* is a strong word," Chuck said encouragingly, putting his hand on Lem's shoulder. "Maybe she just *dislikes* you."

Lem covered his face with his hands again. "Plus there's another guy," he added sadly. "Glar."

Chuck gave Lem's shoulder a squeeze. "You know your problem?" he asked. "It's not Glar. Or Neera. It's *Lem*." He pulled Lem's hands away from his face. "Look at you . . . you're so left-brained. Or is it right-brained? Whatever . . ." The astronaut gave one of Lem's arms a rough wiggle. "You've got to loosen up."

The pep talk didn't work—Lem looked sadder than ever, his shoulders slumping.

Chuck peered down at his digital readout, checking how long he had before the command module in orbit left for Earth without him. "We've got a little time," he decided. "You, my friend, are in luck. The doctor is in!"

The astronaut yanked Lem off the stool and dragged him into the back storeroom. "Me and Green Bean need to talk," he told the others, and shut the door.

The storeroom was filled with cardboard boxes and files on one end, and a cozy office and lounge on the other end. There were more racks of back issues of comics, and older cardboard cutouts of monsters and aliens lining the walls.

Chuck dimmed the lights. He spotted a record player near an overstuffed chair and he selected a mellow, jazzy record. He put the record on the player, but before he dropped the needle arm, he paused. "I have a technical question," Chuck said. "Are you considered ugly on this planet? Because I can't tell."

"No," Lem replied. "I mean . . . I'm okay."

"Good!" said Chuck. He let go of the needle, and the storeroom filled with low, sultry music. Chuck swayed in place and snapped his fingers. "Why do chicks dig me? Because I'm handsome? Because I'm an astronaut? Yes . . . and yes. But it's also because of Chuck Baker's three steps to romance."

Lem plopped down into the overstuffed chair, unsure if he wanted to deal with Chuck's lesson, but also curious to hear his advice.

Suavely, the astronaut strolled over to Lem, acting like he thought he was the hottest guy at a nightclub. "Spot your prey," he instructed. "Make your move. Show no mercy!" He suddenly kneeled down next to Lem, propping up his chin on his hand, with his elbow on the arm of the chair. "Hey, baby, I saw you across the bar," he cooed as though Lem were a beautiful woman. "Are sparks flying or is this place on fire?" Then Chuck released the full wattage of his bright smile and winked.

His stomach churning, Lem pressed himself into the cushions, totally grossed out.

"You're sure you're not ugly, right?" Chuck asked.

Lem licked his lips, which had gone dry. "I think so."

Chuck stood up fully, and before Lem could protest, he pulled him out of the chair and held him close, swaying in a romantic dance. "Baby," Chuck purred, "tomorrow I go up in space, maybe never to return. Let's make our last night one we'll remember!"

Then, as the music swelled, Chuck dipped Lem backward.

That's when the door opened, and Skiff stepped inside the storeroom. Behind him, the two soldiers, Eckle, and Rover all stared at the dancers in shock.

Lem couldn't have been happier to be interrupted. He pulled away from Chuck, smoothed down his squishy hair, and stormed out to the front room.

"We need to get Chuck on TV," Lem said firmly. "I'll be back with a reporter." Narrowing his eyes, Lem pointed at Skiff. "I'm leaving you in charge."

Skiff smiled. As soon as Lem stepped out the door, Skiff ran to the back room and stood self-importantly in the doorway. "You heard him!" he announced. "Things are gonna be different around here! My wish is your command!"

After blinking once, Chuck slammed the storeroom door in his face.

Skiff was disappointed, but then Rover rolled over to him and nuzzled his leg affectionately. Skiff gave the little robot a big smile.

Lem strode down Main Street, heading toward the central TV station on the other side of the square. As he turned the corner, he noticed a commotion in front of the town hall. Glar, Neera, and a bunch of teenagers were protesting the military operation.

Stopping short, Lem considered whether he should continue to the TV station . . . or detour to talk to Neera. It wasn't much of a choice, really—he couldn't stand how badly he'd left things with Neera. Lem marched over to the protesters.

"Neera . . . ," Lem said weakly when he was close enough.

Neera saw him but turned her back on him huffily.

Lem swallowed. "I need to talk to you!" he called in a louder voice.

Neera turned around and glared at him. "I thought you were after the alien," she snapped.

"That's not what's going on," Lem tried to explain.

Neera crossed her arms over her chest. "Then what is?"

Before Lem could reply, Glar stepped up to Neera's side. "*Lem, mysterious Lem*," he sang, "*tell us the secrets of your heart. . . .*"

Lem sighed. He couldn't explain with Glar and the other protesters listening. It would be too embarrassing, and he didn't know what Glar would do if he knew Lem was hiding an alien astronaut in the comic book store. Lem shook his head sadly. "I can't say."

Neera let out a groan. "Lem, I always thought we'd be together," she told him, "but I need someone who doesn't always believe what he's told. Like Glar says . . . the times, they are a different." She turned her back on him again. "Maybe you should go."

With no other options, Lem made a quick decision to put Chuck's love lesson into action. He tried to slink over to Neera as suavely as Chuck had moved, but he felt awkward and clumsy. "Neera," he said in a goofy deep voice. "is this place sparking or is fire making this a night I'll show no mercy? Did I happen to mention I'm not ugly?"

Neera grimaced. "Are you crazy?" She shook her head. "Wow."

Desperately, Lem reached around Neera as though they were dancing, and he tried to lean her backward in a romantic dip. He wasn't sure what he'd done wrong, but he ended up flat on his back, staring up at the cloudy sky. Then Neera's face came into view, looking down at him in confusion.

Glar joined Neera in peering down at Lem, putting his arm around her shoulders. "Is this guy giving you bad vibrations?"

Neera sighed sadly. "Lem was just leaving."

Glar and Neera walked away, leaving Lem lying on the ground.

To make matters worse, the clouds above rumbled, and rocks began to rain down.

Back in the storeroom of the comic book store, Chuck let out a bored yawn. He glanced down at his digital readout—only sixteen hours left before the orbiter took off.

Seeing Chuck yawn, Eckle decided to liven up the situation. He grabbed a toy laser gun off a shelf and pointed it at the astronaut. *"Pew! Pew!"* Eckle yelped, imitating the sound of laser fire. "I got you, alien! Victory or extinction!"

Chuck smiled. Then he jumped up and seized another toy blaster. "Oh, yeah?" he replied, aiming the gun at Eckle. "In space, no one can hear you scream!" He rushed at Eckle, pretending to fire the blaster.

Eckle squealed when Chuck grabbed him, and the young boy squirmed away from the astronaut, giggling.

"Crush, kill, destroy!" Chuck boomed like a movie monster.

Private Vesklin jumped up beside Chuck and saluted. "Master," he said. "We want to be destroyed, too!"

In the store's main room, Skiff noticed that Rover was chirping worriedly beside the window, listening to the sound of the rain of rocks. "You're afraid of a little storm?" Skiff chided the robot. He pulled up the shades to show Rover. "It's nothing, see?"

But Rover wasn't scared of the storm—he was deliriously excited about all the rocks bouncing around outside. His digital readout spun into a blur. Losing control, Rover bounced up and smashed through the window, zooming out into the rocky rain.

Skiff let out a scream. He grabbed a metal umbrella and chased after the robot. "Rover!" he cried. "Sit!"

But Rover was so thrilled that he didn't heed Skiff. The robot probe danced in the falling rocks, scooping up stones with his claws.

"Stay!" Skiff yelled. "Heel?" He was so busy rushing after Rover that he didn't notice the TV reporter standing under an awning next door, sipping a cup of coffee. His news van was parked nearby.

When the reporter saw the alien robot roll away down the street, he spat out a mouthful of coffee in amazement.

The reporter banged on the van's window. When his cameraman slid open the door, the reporter said, "Six o'clock news, here we go." He led the cameraman and his sound guy over to the comic book store, and they peered through the broken window.

Crazy screams and noises were coming from the back room.

"You can't escape the tractor beam!" Chuck hollered. "It's pulling you to your doom!"

The cameraman quickly set up his camera

outside the broken window, aiming it through the ajar storeroom door. He had a perfect view of Chuck from there.

Meanwhile, the television crew's sound guy quietly snuck around the back and jammed his microphone through a small opening in the storeroom's window.

Lem waited out the rain in the park's gazebo. When the falling rocks stopped as suddenly as they had started, he resumed walking toward the TV station. As he reached a corner, he passed by a hardware store, which had dozens of oval TV sets in the storefront window. The TVs were turned to the news, and Lem caught a familiar image out of the corner of his eye.

He backed up to get a better look.

Chuck was live on all the TVs. The astronaut lurched across the comic book store. The movie monster cardboard cutouts behind him made it look like he was the leader of a terrifying alien army. "Soon we will crush the rebel alliance and control the galaxy!" Chuck growled in a scary voice.

Gasping in horror, Lem watched as Vernkot and

Vesklin cheered Chuck's announcement. Behind them, Lem could clearly see racks of comic books.

Lem raced back toward the comic book store. "Skiff!" he screamed.

Chapter 8

When Lem burst into the backroom of the comic book store, he found Chuck, Eckle, and the two soldiers laughing hysterically. "Hey!" Lem interrupted them. "We've got to get out of here now!"

They made it out the back door just as the military arrived and bashed in the front door. Lem, Chuck, and Eckle jumped in the jeep, leaving Vesklin and Vernkot behind.

"It's too dangerous," Lem said, shaking his head as he pushed Eckle out.

"But . . . ," Eckle protested.

A soldier pushed past Vesklin and Vernkot out the back door. "You there!" he hollered at Lem. "Stop!"

Lem drove out of the parking lot as fast as the space jeep would go, while Eckle ducked down behind the garbage cans to hide. In his rearview mirror, Lem could see dozens of soldiers teeming out of the comic book store. A few of them aimed their rifles and took shots at the escaping jeep.

Out on the street, Skiff had finally caught up to Rover, whose two metal arms were overflowing with rocks collected from the rain. "Don't ever run off like that!" Skiff scolded the robot. "What if they took you to the pound? How would I find you?"

Skiff froze as Lem and Chuck whizzed by at top speed in the jeep. Then a fleet of army jeeps raced by, chasing after Lem and Chuck.

"Oh, boy," Skiff said worriedly, and he took off after them.

Rover inspected his pile of rocks. After considering it a moment longer, he let out a loud whine and dropped the rocks. He dashed after Skiff on his six wheels.

Lem careened the jeep swiftly around a corner . . . and screeched to a halt. A giant floating tank was blocking the road ahead. It pivoted its giant gun to aim at them.

Without hesitation, Lem and Chuck bailed out of the jeep.

"We better run!" Chuck gasped.

He and Lem sprinted toward an alley.

Boom!

The tank fired a massive artillery shell, and the jeep exploded in a huge fireball.

Lem and Chuck stumbled from the force of the blast, but quickly regained their footing. "Let's move!" Lem yelped.

Coming through the smoke from the explosion, troops of soldiers ran toward Chuck and Lem. The teenager and the astronaut hurried into an alley, but dozens of soldiers appeared on the other end of the short passageway, marching toward them.

Lem and Chuck turned around again, but the soldiers had blocked off their exit. There was no escape.

Behind the soldiers, Skiff and Rover skidded to a halt when they saw that their friends were surrounded. Skiff backed up slowly, not knowing how to help.

Rover inspected the situation, and then rotated his head to look for a solution. He spotted a low truck parked nearby. The robot quickly zoomed up the side of the truck and rolled onto its roof. Rover raised all of his arms and antennae, and crouched down in his most menacing pose. The leftover smoke from the explosion swirled around him, making him look even scarier. Then Rover let out a high-pitched whistle to get the soldiers' attention.

Rover's plan worked. A soldier pointed at him. "Look out!" he hollered. "The monster!"

All the soldiers on the near end of the alley rushed toward Rover. The robot tried to back off the truck to safety, but two soldiers grabbed him from behind, and the others piled on.

"Rover?" Skiff cried, watching his friend get captured. He shook his fists at the sky. *Noooooo!* he wailed.

Lem and Chuck were worried for the safety of

the brave robot, but they saw their chance to escape—and they took it. They dashed out of the alley behind the soldiers, turned the corner, and raced toward a car parked in the shadows. Lem yanked open the door, and he and Chuck ducked inside the hovering vehicle.

"Quick," Chuck ordered Lem, who was in the driver's seat, "hotwire the car!"

Lem stared at the astronaut blankly. "Um . . . ," he said. "Do what to the car?"

Chuck quickly switched places with Lem, and then reached under the dashboard to pull out a few wires. He connected their bare copper ends. A blue spark flared up, and the car engine started. "When are you green goobers going to evolve?"

Pressing down on the gas pedal, Chuck drove the car down the suburban street, away from the soldiers.

Skiff turned around just in time to see his friends driving toward the hills, where the observatory peeked through the trees. With a sad sigh, he turned back to watch Rover being dumped into the back of a truck, which then pulled away down the street.

Keeping his distance, Skiff followed the truck a short distance until it stopped in front of the comic book store. Teams of military scientists in hazmat suits had wrapped the whole store in plastic sheeting, and were still busy sanitizing the inside of it. Skiff watched helplessly as soldiers carried Rover into the plastic-wrapped store and the scientists sealed the exit behind them.

Skiff felt a tug on his arm.

It was Eckle, gazing wide-eyed up at him. "Where's Rover?"

"Why did he do it?" Skiff moaned. "I was gonna teach him to fetch!"

Eckle let Skiff hug him and sob on his shoulder. Behind him, the TV reporter stood across from the store and spoke looking into a camera, as a big flatbed military truck was coming up the road, transporting Chuck's spaceship.

"The flying saucer is going to an undisclosed location to be taken apart and studied," the reporter announced to his audience. "This reporter is now going to reveal to you where that location is." Then he squinted and pressed his earpiece as a message came in. "This reporter has just been told that if I do that, *I* will be taken apart and studied."

Lem and Chuck reached the observatory without incident. Lem let them into the empty building and they hurried up to the high balcony to get a view of what was happening in town.

In the distance, they could clearly see the army flatbed truck carting Chuck's spaceship onto the highway toward the desert.

With a sigh, Chuck checked the digital readout on his space suit. He had only about twelve hours before the orbiter went back to Earth. "Great," Chuck muttered sarcastically. "Perfect! John Glenn goes around the world . . . he's a senator for life! I went across the universe . . . I should be a governor, minimum! But no . . . I'm marooned on this stupid rock!" He groaned, and stomped back inside the observatory.

Lem followed Chuck inside, and started shutting

the window shades as though it were still his normal life and he was closing down for the night. The fact that his life was no longer even close to normal irritated Lem so much that he turned on Chuck angrily. "This *stupid rock* is my home," he snapped. "Or it *was* until you came along and ruined everything! I want my life back! Unless maybe there's something *else* you want to ruin!"

Storming around a corner, Lem bumped headlong into the curator. The older man also had been closing window shades for the night.

Lem and the curator blinked at each other.

"Who's this?" Chuck asked.

Lem shook his head ruefully. "My boss."

Before the curator could protest, Chuck and Lem grabbed him, dragged him down to the break room, and gently stuffed him into Lem's locker.

"I'm sorry, Sir," Lem apologized to his boss, who looked horribly uncomfortable in the narrow locker. "It's just for one night . . . a week at the most." He forced a smile at the curator. "I hope this won't affect our working relationship." Then Lem closed the locker door.

Inside the locker, the curator knocked politely.

Lem opened the locker, and a picture of Neera fell out onto the floor.

The curator held up a piece of paper on which he'd written the word FIRED in red letters.

Lem nodded, unsurprised, and shut the door again.

Wearily, Lem rested his forehead against the locker door. He got angrier and angrier as he thought about how his whole life had been destroyed just by the bad luck of a spaceship landing in his neighborhood and then running into Chuck at the observatory. Everything had gone wrong since he had decided to help Chuck! It all seemed so unfair.

He whirled around to face Chuck. "This is all just great!" he snarled. "Why don't you just harvest my organs and get it over with!" He stormed out of the break room.

Lem strode into the dark planetarium. He felt

so irritated that he needed something to calm him down, and he knew the best thing would be to look at the stars. After starting the projector, Lem plopped down into one of the cushioned seats to stare up at the vastness of galaxies overhead.

After a few minutes of stargazing, Lem winced when he heard footsteps entering the planetarium. He still was in no mood to deal with Chuck.

"Kid . . . ?" Chuck asked softly. "Lem?"

When Lem didn't reply, Chuck sat down next to him.

Lem bit his lip, still staring up at the stars on the domed ceiling.

After a long, awkward moment of silence between them, Chuck cleared his throat and pointed up at a faraway star system. "You're looking right at my home," Chuck said. "See that star, the little red one? Circling that star is a planet called Earth. It's about twenty billion miles away."

Despite his anger, Lem was amazed by the distance Chuck had traveled. "Space is that big?"

"What, are you kidding?" Chuck replied. "There

are billions of galaxies. And each galaxy has billions of stars. Next to that our planets are just dust in the wind."

Lem slumped deeper into his chair. Chuck's speech had just made him feel small and miserable instead of angry. "So . . . nothing I knew was right."

"You knew about Neera," Chuck said. He held up the picture of her that had fallen out of Lem's locker, and smiled at it in the dim light. "I mean, *look* at her. Lose the antennae, get some plastic surgery . . . she's a hottie."

Lem lowered his head, looking away from the photo. "I don't have the Right Stuff like you."

Chuck sighed. "Kid, I never had the Right Stuff," he confessed. "I'm a button pusher. Spam in a can. I don't even fly the ship—it's all automatic. I only got this far on charm." He raised his strong chin. "That, and my rugged good looks." He shook Lem's shoulder gently. "You risked everything to help a stranger from another world. *You're* the one with the Right Stuff."

Slowly, Lem raised his head to meet Chuck's gaze, his eyes tearing up.

The planetarium was suddenly flooded with bright light. Lem and Chuck turned around in their chairs to see who had come in.

Skiff and Eckle were standing in the doorway, peering into the planetarium.

"Guys!" Chuck called out happily.

"There you are!" Eckle cheered. He and Skiff rushed over and met Chuck and Lem in the aisle. They all grinned at one another.

"Great hiding spot," Skiff said. "Let's stay here."

Eckle shook his head. "No way! Let's go fight the army!"

"How's your species at hiding?" Skiff asked Chuck. "Can you change your skin to our color?"

Chuck didn't respond to Skiff's silliness.

"Your call, Captain Baker," Eckle told the astronaut. "What's it going to be? Fight or hide?"

Chuck pressed his lips together, thinking about the options.

"Neither!" Lem said firmly. "I tell you what it's going to be. We're going to go get Chuck back to his ship. Skiff, you must be right about Base 9. That has to be where they have the ship."

"But we don't know where it is," Eckle reminded him.

Chuck scratched his chin, and his eyes suddenly lit up. "Yes we do!" he said. "Rover found me! He's also programmed to find my ship." He peered around Eckle and Skiff, looking out the doorway. "Where *is* Rover?"

With a sob, Skiff collapsed on the floor and began to weep. "It's too painful to talk about!"

Eckle patted Skiff on the shoulder. "It's okay," he said consolingly. Then he looked up at Lem and Chuck. "They've got Rover at the comic book store."

"Then we've got to go get him!" Lem declared.

Skiff stood up, his tears gone. "Hold on," he said. "The whole army's looking for you two. You can't just stroll through town."

Lem nodded. He started to pace down the aisle, wracking his brain to think up a way they could get to the comic book store without being spotted by the military. It was impossible to hide an alien astronaut like Chuck, unless—

Struck with an idea, Lem whirled around. "That new movie . . . doesn't it open tonight?" he asked Skiff and Eckle.

Skiff glanced at Eckle, who nodded. "Yeah," Skiff replied. "Why?"

Lem smiled.

Chapter 9

Back in town, Chuck, Eckle, Skiff, and Lem peered around the side of a building toward the movie theater. A crowd of kids and parents had gathered under the marquee. A lot of the kids were in homemade alien outfits for the *Humaniacs III* costume contest. Some of the kids entering the contest were dressed like crazy monsters, but others looked basically like humans.

Lem, too, was dressed as a human, wearing a helmet and a shirt. Chuck was wearing his space suit, with his mirrored helmet covering his face.

They had to pass the movie theater on the way to the comic book store. Lem took note of a couple of soldiers guarding the gathering. With a deep breath, he led his friends down the sidewalk, through the crowd.

They walked by the TV announcer, who was giving a report into a camera. "The residents of Glipforg, undaunted by alien invaders, are bravely going about their normal routines," the reporter told his audience.

From inside the open doors of the theater, Eckle spotted his teacher onstage, giving directions to the people in costume. "Humaniacs to my left! Machiniacs to my right!" she instructed. "Fleshivores and brain eaters in the middle!"

Just as they had gotten past the theater, Lem and Chuck each felt a hand on his shoulder.

Lem nearly screamed. He whirled around and came face-to-face with another teacher.

The teacher peered at Lem and Chuck through her big round glasses. "Great costumes!" she told them. "You two are finalists." She pointed into the theater. "Get up onstage!"

"We're not here to enter the contest," Lem said.

The teacher raised her eyebrows. "Then why are

you dressed like aliens?"

Her question attracted the attention of the soldiers, who glared at Lem and Chuck suspiciously.

Lem glanced around nervously, and saw that a few more soldiers were heading over to the theater. He smiled at the teacher. "We're here to *win* the contest!" he declared.

"Yeah!" Chuck agreed. "We're going to win." He held up his gloved hand to Lem. "Give me five!"

Everyone around fell silent, staring at Chuck.

"Five?" the teacher asked.

Chuck nodded his helmet. "Because I'm an alien, right?" he said quickly. He slapped Lem's four-fingered hand with his five-fingered glove.

Letting out a sigh, Lem followed the teacher into the theater, with Chuck trailing behind. There were even more soldiers guarding the inside of the theater. Lem gave a desperate glance backward at Skiff, who was still outside.

Near Skiff, Lem spotted Neera, Glar, and the teenage protesters climbing out of Glar's car. They were getting ready to protest, carrying signs that read MAKE LOVE, NOT GALACTIC WAR; HUG AN ALIEN; and HAVE A NICE INVASION.

The teacher led Lem and Chuck onto the stage and left them in a lineup of kids wearing costumes. She headed over to the microphone and tapped it. "Welcome to the *Humaniacs III* costume contest," the teacher announced. "Let's hear it for the finalists!"

The crowd in the theater cheered. Lem's parents, who were in the audience, stared at him, surprised to see him up onstage.

Lem leaned over to whisper to Chuck, "What are we supposed to do?"

Lifting his helmet just slightly, Chuck peered out at the crowd and smiled slyly. "Give them their daily minimum dose of Chuck," he replied.

Chuck secured his helmet again. He stepped forward and waved to the crowd, posing in his space suit. "Hello, Humaniacs!" he called out.

The audience applauded, impressed by what they

thought was an incredibly realistic costume.

Lem shook his head in disbelief as Chuck seemed to float by doing the moonwalk, but the crowd gasped in awe and then cheered wildly.

Chuck started doing the twist in the middle of the stage. He motioned for Lem to join him, but Lem shook his head.

The crowd cheered again, and Chuck grabbed Lem's arm and pulled him to the front of the stage, forcing him to dance along.

Feeling incredibly embarrassed, Lem awkwardly bobbed along to the music. He slowly grew more comfortable up onstage, and finally busted out a fancy dance move.

The audience erupted with cheers and applause.

Lem smiled. He was starting to have fun. When Chuck dropped to the floorboards and performed a hip-hop spin, Lem laughed and joined him, to the delight of the crowd.

Down in the audience, Eckle heard a familiar mechanical whine. His eyes widened when he saw Rover rolling into the theater.

The little robot was followed by a troop of soldiers.

Eckle waved to Chuck and Lem, trying to get their attention. But the song had ended, and they were busy holding up their arms in triumph, basking in the cheers of the crowd.

Rover buzzed down the aisle, applauding for Lem and Chuck with his claws. He stopped beside a little girl.

The girl turned to smile at Rover . . . and then noticed that she was smiling at an alien robot.

She let out an ear-piercing scream.

Everyone turned to look. When they saw Rover, they screamed, too, and began to push their way out of the theater in a panic.

The soldiers took that as their cue to march toward the stage.

"How did they find us?" Lem asked.

"They must've figured out how to use Rover to track me down!" Chuck replied.

They looked around the theater for a way to escape, but the aisles were full of panicking people bumping into one another in terror. Soldiers pushed through the crowd, grabbing people in alien costumes and ripping off their masks, trying to find Chuck.

In the back of the theater, Skiff and Eckle waved to Lem. They pointed to a side-door exit that was reasonably clear of frenzied people.

Lem pulled Chuck toward the side of the theater, and headed for that exit.

Seeing the pandemonium that he'd caused, Rover whined worriedly, and tried to zip through the crowd, but kept banging into people's legs. Finally, a space cleared, and he rolled toward the exit.

Someone was standing directly in Rover's way. It was General Grawl, glaring down at the robot through his dark sunglasses.

The general motioned to his troops, and they hurried over to recapture Rover.

Barging through the stampeding crowd, the chunky army captain made his way over to General Grawl. "All these costumes . . ." He panted. "How do we find the alien?"

Grawl scanned the crowd and smiled grimly.

"Simple, Captain," he replied. "Like us, the alien is in uniform." He pointed to Chuck across the theater, who had a red, white, and blue flag patch on his shoulder.

Chuck and Lem were getting closer to the side exit. They passed by Neera, and for a quick moment, Lem met Neera's surprised gaze.

On the general's orders, the troops moved swiftly to block the side exit. They swarmed around Chuck and Lem, pushing everyone else away.

Eckle watched the soldiers jamming Rover into what looked like a big dog carrier. His heart went out to the brave little robot, and he wished there was something he could do to help. Then he noticed a boxy alien costume with wheels that had been abandoned near the carrier. When Eckle squinted, the costume looked a little like Rover. "Hmm," he murmured.

General Grawl strode over to where Chuck and Lem were being held by the soldiers. The short, big-headed scientist, Professor Kipple, stood beside the general.

Realizing that there was no escape, Chuck took off his helmet. Soldiers gasped in shock as his pink, alien face was revealed.

Neera stared at Chuck in astonishment and then looked over at Lem. She shook her head sadly as she realized what Lem had been up to the whole time. He hadn't been hunting aliens—he'd been protecting one!

General Grawl whipped off his sunglasses and inspected Chuck, obviously displeased. "Look at it, Professor," the general told Kipple. "It's hideous! And that smell!"

"Hey," Chuck protested, "you try wearing the same suit for three weeks."

Peering at Chuck through his monocle, Kipple got close to the astronaut, examining Chuck's head. "What a remarkable brain you must have." He pointed up at his ears. "An incision here . . . and here . . . and it should pop right out."

Chuck's face crumpled in horror, and Lem and his friends all looked terrified. Even General Grawl looked grossed out by the professor's gruesome announcement.

"You're making a mistake!" Lem called, struggling against the soldiers holding him. "He's friendly!"

Kipple turned to peer at Lem. "The poor boy's obviously a zombie," he declared. "I'll remove his brain, too."

That shocked Lem. His eyes grew wide with fear. Neera gasped, and his mother burst into tears nearby.

"Chuck," Lem said, begging the astronaut to help.

Chuck knew he had to do something. With a burst of brute force, Chuck broke free of the soldiers holding him and rushed toward Lem. As loudly as he could, he started making a high-pitched science-fiction noise with his lips.

Hmmmmmmmmmmmmmmmmmmmmmmmmm!

That scared everyone in the theater, except Professor Kipple. Everyone else took a step backward.

Chuck held out his arms like a rampaging

monster, and tottered toward Lem, making weird hypnotic motions. "You are no longer needed, slave!" he intoned in a deep, robotic voice. "I release you! Return to your puny life!" Then Chuck put his hands on either side of Lem's head as if to squeeze his brain. Leaning close, the astronaut whispered into Lem's ear, "Kid, I'm going down anyway. No need for you to go with me. Thanks for everything."

With a final ear-splitting screech, Chuck let go of Lem's head, flicking his wrists dramatically.

When Chuck stepped back, the crowd just stared in shocked silence. Then Lem's parents rushed over and grabbed him in a hug.

Chuck headed back to the soldiers and let himself be recaptured.

"How about it, Professor?" General Grawl asked.

Kipple strode over to Lem and inspected him with his monocle. "Do you still believe the alien is friendly?" he demanded.

Lem didn't answer right away. He looked around at his friends and family first.

His parents were staring at him with hope in their eyes. Neera shook her head. Skiff mouthed the word *no*. Chuck offered Lem a sad smile and also shook his head.

Finally, Lem looked down at his sneakers. "No," he said.

"This boy is free!" Professor Kipple crowed.

The soldiers and onlookers cheered, and Lem's friends and his parents heaved sighs of relief. Lem didn't feel like celebrating at all—his stomach ached with miserable guilt.

"All right," General Grawl stated. "Let's get these aliens to Base 9." He put his sunglasses back on. "Not that it exists."

Seeing the terribly sad look on Chuck's face as the soldiers led him away made Lem choke back a heartsick sob.

Lem's parents led him outside, following the soldiers. They watched as Chuck was loaded onto an army truck, the dog carrier placed beside him. Grawl climbed with Kipple into a nearby Humvee and closed the door behind them.

As the truck and the Humvee drove away, people gathered around Lem, blocking his last glimpse of Chuck.

The next morning, Lem's parents brought him to the observatory, where a press conference had been hastily set up. Lem waited backstage behind a temporary backdrop while the TV reporter introduced him to a live audience.

"We're here to honor a youngster who survived a harrowing ordeal with the alien monster," the reporter announced. "Lem, come on out!"

The people in the audience applauded. In the crowd were many familiar faces, including Neera, Eckle, Skiff, Eckle's parents, Chief Gorloc, the mailman, a few teachers, and the observatory curator.

Backstage beside his parents, Lem stared straight ahead like a zombie and didn't move.

"Son?" his father prompted.

His eyes snapping into focus, Lem nodded glumly. He headed past the curtain to sit by the TV reporter.

"Lem," the reporter said, "I understand you'll be working right here at the observatory after you graduate, teaching about the mysteries of space. Give us a preview of what we'll learn."

Before saying anything, Lem peered out beyond the lights at the audience, feeling extremely uncomfortable. He saw Neera smile and the curator nodding his head. Lem licked his lips, which had gone dry. "Well," he began, reciting what he'd learned from his old astronomy book, "we know everything about our universe. It's five hundred miles long."

"Five hundred miles!" the reporter repeated in amazement, and the audience murmured, sounding impressed by that information.

Lem nodded. "And have you ever tried counting the stars?" he asked in a flat voice. "Don't bother, there's too many. More than one thousand."

"One thousand!" the reporter said. "Remarkable."

The audience applauded the wrong facts Lem had just recited, and the sound snapped him out of his fog. "I can't . . . ," he muttered.

"Excuse me?" the reporter asked.

Lem shook his head, sitting up straighter and looking directly at the newscaster. "No," he said firmly. "Space isn't five hundred miles. It's so much bigger than we can imagine." He gazed out at the audience. "There are billions of galaxies," he told them passionately, "and each galaxy has billions of stars. Next to that, our planet is just . . ."

Seeing that the audience members were shifting uncomfortably in their seats, Lem let his words trail off. He stood up. "Excuse me," he said, and walked off the set.

Chapter 10

Outside the observatory, the morning was bright and sunny. Lem found a blue convertible parked on the street and climbed inside it. He stuck his head under the dashboard to see the wires underneath.

Neera had followed him outside, and she hurried over to the convertible. "Lem, I know I was kind of harsh before," she said, too softly for him to hear. "I'm really sorry."

When she got no reply, Neera narrowed her eyes. "Well, at least say *something*!"

Startled by the sound of her voice, Lem banged his head on the dashboard. "Ouch!" he complained, sitting up and rubbing his head. "Oh, hi, Neera." He peered under the dashboard again and touched two wires together, starting the car's ignition. The engine purred.

"What are you doing?" Neera asked.

"It's called hotwiring," Lem explained. "It's how they start cars on Earth."

Neera smiled, impressed. Then she glanced away and bit her lip. "Lem . . ."

Gulping at the tone of her voice, Lem sat up straight. "Yeah, Neera?"

Before Neera could continue, Skiff came running over to the convertible. "Lem!" he complained. "You left everyone hanging!"

Lem shrugged, and then gripped the steering wheel with determination in his eyes. "I'm going to go find Chuck."

"But how?" Skiff asked. "We don't have Rover to track him. . . ."

"Yes we do!" Eckle called. He hustled over to the car, with Rover rolling along behind him.

Skiff screamed in happiness, throwing up his arms. He launched himself at the little robot and grabbed Rover in a big hug. "Rover!" he screeched. "You're alive!" Skiff laughed deliriously when Rover nuzzled his cheek with his head.

"I pulled a switcheroo!" Eckle explained to his friends proudly.

Skiff raised his head from hugging Rover and gave Eckle a happy thumbs-up.

Lem smiled—things were finally improving. He leaned out of the car, getting closer to Rover. "Can you find Chuck, boy?" he asked the robot. "Where's Chuck?"

Extending his head as high as it would go, Rover swiveled around, scanning the area as though he were trying to pick up Chuck's scent. Suddenly his tracking light blinked. Rover focused on Lem and nodded.

Skiff climbed into the back of the convertible. "Let's go!" he cheered.

"You're going with me?" Lem asked, surprised.

"Yeah," Neera cut in as she hurried around

to the passenger side and hopped inside the car. "I'm in, too."

"Me, too!" Eckle said.

"All right!" Lem exclaimed with a smile.

As Lem drove the convertible through town, he banked around the park and neared the town hall. Glar and his teenage posse were in their usual place, but this time the teens were taking apart their signs and giving up the protest.

As the convertible passed the town hall, Lem heard Glar strumming his guitar and singing, "*We tried to change the world, but ran out of rhymes.*" He suddenly stopped and asked his followers, "What rhymes with *rhymes*?"

Lem stopped the car and backed up, struck with an idea. "Hey, Glar!" he called. "How would you like a cause you can really sing about?"

"Dig!" Glar replied happily. When everyone just stared at him blankly, Glar tried again. "Cool!" Again, he got only confused looks. "Far out!" he tried. When the others still stared at him blankly, Glar dropped his hippie voice and said, "What I mean to say is, that would be really desirable."

Behind him, Glar's group of teenage protesters cheered and smiled.

"Take the desert road," Lem instructed Glar. "We'll meet up ahead." Then Lem shifted gears on the hovering convertible and drove out of town.

The sun was high in the sky when Lem and his friends were led by Rover to a gas station deep in the desert. The gas station looked abandoned and dusty, with broken-down pumps. A tall sign loomed over the parking lot.

Lem stopped the car, and everybody got out to look around. Outside the gas station was nothing but empty, sandy desert.

Rover zoomed around in circles, his red light flashing rapidly.

"He thinks we found Chuck," Skiff said apologetically.

Lem nodded and looked out at the empty gas station. There was absolutely no sign of any secret base. "Hang on, Chuck," he whispered. "We'll find you."

Eckle wandered over to the station's store; and Lem, Neera, and Skiff followed along. Inside, the place was dilapidated and rundown, with dusty counters, broken display cases, and empty magazine racks. It looked like nobody had entered the store in years.

"Hello!" Lem called. "Anyone here?"

A sudden rattling sound behind him made Lem jump. He whirled around to see Skiff whacking his hand against an old display case while pulling on its door with his other hand. He was trying to get a lonely old candy bar.

"Skiff, what are you doing?" Lem asked, annoyed.

"No one's around," Skiff replied. "I'm not going to get caught." He managed to yank the door open and grabbed the candy bar.

The second that Skiff picked up the package, low, ominous tremors shook the ground. Rumbling echoed across the desert. The gas station began to shake violently.

Holding on to the counter for support, Lem glared at Skiff, but his expression softened when Neera clasped his arm.

Skiff let go of the candy bar. He scrambled to pull coins out of his pocket. "I'm paying!" he cried, holding up the coins.

An ear-splitting screech sounded from the parking lot. Lem, Neera, Skiff, and Eckle rushed to the gas station's window and peered out.

Their mouths dropped open in shock as the tall gas station sign slowly began to lean to one side. It wasn't falling—the ground beneath it was raising up. The sign was *rotating*.

As the sign sunk underground, the flip side of it emerged, revealing a long ramp leading down.

Lem and his friends gaped in amazement.

"The thing with the . . ." Eckle gasped. "Went over the . . . Wow!"

They exited the gas station's store and walked slowly over to the ramp. Along its edges there were landing lights leading downward.

Lem peeked over the edge and saw a road leading

to a massive army base hidden below the ground. It was a brightly lit underground military city, two hundred feet below a reinforced concrete ceiling, teeming with vehicles and soldiers. The base itself had high walls and looked heavily guarded.

"Base 9?" Lem asked.

Skiff nodded. "This is amazing," he gasped. "I was right again!"

Rover chirped excitedly.

"How do we get in without being seen?" Neera asked.

At that moment, Glar arrived in his battered car and pulled into the gas station's parking lot. Glar and his friends waved and smiled.

Lem returned Glar's smile.

Lem had an idea.

Chapter  11

With his followers in the car, Glar drove down underground. The subterranean space around Base 9 was vast, and the ceiling high above.

Glar and his friends hopped out of the car. The teenagers carried signs with slogans such as LET THE MAN GO!; A BRAIN IS A TERRIBLE THING TO WASTE!; and MAKE LOVE, NOT INTERSTELLAR WAR!

They gathered behind Glar, who slung a harmonica around his neck and then picked up his guitar.

Glar strummed the guitar loudly, getting the soldiers' attention. He hummed into the harmonica, but he let the music fade away when he saw the soldiers glaring at him. "Uh . . . is being here against the rules?" Glar asked.

The soldiers hollered and charged at Glar and his friends.

The teens turned and ran back up the ramp.

As soon as the soldiers ran past, chasing Glar, Lem and his group snuck out from behind Glar's car. "C'mon," Lem urged, and they all hurried toward Base 9's main buildings.

Near the front gate, they peeked around it to check out the soldiers guarding the entrance.

Lem had no idea how to get past the guards. But before Lem could admit defeat, Eckle tapped him on the shoulder. The young boy pointed out an air vent he found.

Rover used his tools to unscrew the vent grate from the wall, and then he led the team into a dark, dusty ventilation shaft. As the robot rolled through the maze of narrow metal tunnels, his light blinked faster as the group got closer to Chuck.

Rover seemed to know exactly where he was going. Lem's knees hurt from crawling on the metal floor of the shaft by the time Rover stopped in front of another grate.

The little robot pushed open the grate and dropped into a large, dimly lit room. Lem and the others scrambled out of the vent to follow him.

They found themselves in a wide, circular space filled with display cases and vats full of glowing liquid. Each one exhibited an alien object that had fallen from the sky.

The group stopped to peer at a hideous alien, a pulsating pod, a floating brain, a meteorite with a throbbing blob oozing out of it, a laser gun attached to a severed robotic arm, and a dented old license plate that read NEW JERSEY.

"See?" Skiff hissed. "I told you they knew about life on other planets!"

Rover didn't waste any time in the display room. He rolled out through a doorway and pointed down the corridor toward another ventilation shaft up ahead.

"This way," Lem said to his friends.

Entering the hall, they were all relieved to find it

was dark but empty. They ran after Rover, who had already disappeared down the corridor.

"Rover, wait!" Lem called. He caught up to the robot just as the floor collapsed under them and they all tumbled into a small, dark storeroom.

The floor of the storeroom had a small grill set in it, and through the metal mesh, Lem could see a brightly lit operating room beneath them.

Lem's eyes widened as he saw Chuck without his space suit on, tied to a peanut-shaped operating table in the room below. Then he gasped as Professor Kipple approached Chuck's head, holding out a buzzing saw.

Rover shoved the grill with his claws and it collapsed. Rover, Lem, Skiff, and Eckle all fell down into the operating room, landing hard on the floor.

Professor Kipple ignored the interruption. He extended the saw's whirling blade toward Chuck's skull and pressed down. Chuck screamed.

Whirrrrrrrrrrr!

Instead of cutting Chuck's head, the saw blade buzzed against Rover's claw. The robot had stuck it in the way just in time.

Kipple dropped the saw and backed up to the other side of the operating room.

Lem and Neera rushed over and untied Chuck. He sat up on the table and gave them a big hug.

"Good work, Rover!" Chuck told the robot. He smiled at Lem and Neera. "Guys, this is so Luke Skywalker of you!" he gushed. "By the way, you're not brother and sister, right?"

Lem and Neera shook their heads in confusion.

"How much time is left?" Eckle asked.

Chuck checked his digital readout—there were twenty-five minutes left. With a smile, Chuck hopped off the table and flipped a switch on Rover's back.

Rover's tracking light started flashing again.

"Rover will take us right to my ship," Chuck explained.

They all followed the robot out of the operating room and down a couple of corridors, until they reached an elevator. They took it up a few floors, and the doors opened onto a dark, massively wide hangar deck.

Rover zoomed into the darkness, and the rest of the team carefully followed him into the room. Before they had taken a few steps, rows of automatic lights flashed on, and a floodlight illuminated Chuck's spaceship in the center of the hangar deck.

"My ship!" Chuck cheered. "Way to go, kid!" He gave Eckle a gentle punch on the shoulder.

Eckle found a control panel hanging from a long chain. He pressed a button, and the deck began to vibrate. Overhead, the domed roof split down the middle, opening up on to the night sky.

Lem reached the spaceship right after Rover. He felt around the edge of the closed hatch, but saw no way to open it.

Beep-boop!

Lights flashed, and the hatch began to slide open. Lem glanced back at Chuck, who was holding a little remote, which had unlocked the door.

Chuck strode purposefully toward the hatch.

Before he reached it, a deep voice shouted, "Step away from the flying saucer and put your hands in the air!"

Everyone turned to see General Grawl advancing into the hangar, followed by Professor Kipple, and a big troop of soldiers. The soldiers' rifles were all aimed at Chuck. In a flash, Chuck, Lem, and his friends were surrounded.

General Grawl stopped in front of Chuck. He held up an oval device with two buttons on it—one green and one red. "This thing here will set the whole base to auto-destruct," the general said. "There was never a chance you'd get away." He pressed the green button, and stacks of explosives all around the hangar began to hum, ready and armed.

"You'd destroy the whole base just to get me?" Chuck asked in disbelief.

"That's sick!" Neera added.

Chuck couldn't help smiling a little. "Actually," he muttered, "it's kind of flattering. . . ."

"Sick, young lady," Grawl answered Neera, "is helping the enemy of your world!" His mouth twisted with disgust. "Sick is befriending a creature that's so completely . . . different! Sick is—" He pointed at Chuck. "Well, *look*, it's right in front of you!" The general stepped back and nodded at Kipple. "I'm sorry, Professor," he said, "it's too dangerous to let the alien live another minute."

Before he could second-guess himself, Lem stepped in front of Chuck. He nodded at General Grawl and approached him carefully. "General, I know what you're afraid of," Lem said. "I understand. I used to be afraid of it, too."

Lem took another step toward the general, getting closer. "It's not Chuck," he continued. "It's not aliens or monsters. It's something even scarier . . . the unknown. I've spent my whole life running from it. And I think maybe you have, too."

Getting even closer to Grawl, Lem swallowed nervously, but was encouraged when he saw the general lowering his gun slightly. "The unknown isn't something to be afraid of," Lem said. He smiled at Chuck. "It can be your best friend."

Lem turned back to face the general, shuffling closer and closer to him as he spoke. "And just when you think it means the end of everything you know . . . it's really just the beginning."

Then Lem grabbed the base-destruct device and jammed his finger down on the red button.

Everybody stared in silent shock. Nobody could believe what Lem had just done.

A piercing alarm broke the silence.

"Base destruct, two minutes," a robotic voice said calmly over the loudspeakers.

Chapter 12

The soldiers behind General Grawl shifted worriedly, their expressions filling with dawning horror.

Lem waved his hand at Professor Kipple, who was still gaping at the destruction device in the general's hand. "What are you looking at?" Lem shouted at the professor. "Run!"

Kipple turned and fled the hangar. The soldiers raced after him, leaving General Grawl behind.

Grawl narrowed his eyes at Lem. Then he raised his gun and aimed it right between the teenager's eyes.

Thinking quickly, Eckle pushed a heavy iron hook on a swinging chain toward General Grawl.

The hook bashed the gun out of the general's hand.

The gun tumbled to the floor . . . and fired.

The bullet whizzed across the room and slammed into a stack of explosives in the corner.

Boom!

The explosives detonated, shaking the walls. The hangar's ceiling trembled and crumbled. A chunk of plaster broke loose and fell right on top of General Grawl.

Grawl crumpled to the floor, knocked out.

"Everyone on board the ship!" Chuck hollered. "Let's go!"

Lem, Neera, Skiff, Eckle, and Rover all dashed through the hatch into the spaceship. Chuck glanced back at the fallen general, but quickly decided to hurry into the spaceship.

Chuck pulled on his spare space suit in a hurry. Then he bolted out the hatch, heading for the general.

Skiff and Lem both poked their heads out of the hatch. "What are you doing?" Skiff cried.

"I can't leave him here!" Chuck answered, dragging the general toward the ship.

Skiff shook his head in disbelief. "Why not?"

"Because he's got the Right Stuff," Lem replied with a smile.

Explosions flared up all across the hangar. Lem and Skiff lost sight of the astronaut in the blaze.

As the seconds dragged on, Lem bit his lip. Where was Chuck?

Finally, Chuck lumbered through a wall of fire, carrying the unconscious General Grawl in his arms.

As Chuck made it onto the ship, the loudspeaker announced, "Base destruct, one minute."

While Lem and Skiff shut the hatch, Chuck sat down in his chair and started flicking switches, turning on all the systems. There wasn't time to start up the autopilot, and Chuck grimaced.

"What's the matter now?" Lem asked nervously.

"I'm going to have to pilot this bucket," he replied grimly. He pressed more buttons, sweat dripping down his forehead.

Finally, Chuck pulled a big lever, and the ship rumbled as it powered up and started its ignition stage.

"Base destruct," the loudspeaker voice said, "ten seconds." Then it counted down the final seconds. "Nine . . . eight . . ."

Neera, Lem, Skiff, and Eckle quickly sat down as the engines rumbled, flaring with flame.

Slowly . . . too slowly . . . the spaceship began to lift off the deck.

"She's heavy!" Chuck cried. He yanked back on the throttle as the ship rose higher, starting to pick up momentum.

"Four . . . ," the loudspeaker voice counted down. "Three . . . two . . ."

Outside the base by the gas station, Glar and his friends stood in the parking lot, waiting for any sign of the rescue party. They had already seen troops of soldiers, scientists, and other base personnel stream out of the base in panic, but they hadn't recognized any of their friends.

And then the ground was rocked by rumbling and detonations below. Glar stumbled backward as the desert sands suddenly spewed up and a massive explosion ruptured the ground. A wide jet of flame burst out of the hole like a volcano. Glar and his friends gaped in horror—nobody could have survived a blast like that. . . .

But then Glar spotted the NASA spaceship zooming through the sky just ahead of the explosion, soaring to safety.

Glar and the teenagers cheered and danced around the parking lot, celebrating wildly.

Chuck couldn't help a wide grin from crossing his face as he steered the capsule into outer space.

Through the windows, the blue sky faded as they left the planet's atmosphere, replaced by a gorgeous panorama of inky darkness studded with twinkling stars.

Everyone looked out the windows, gaping in awe at the stellar view.

"You guys should check this out," Chuck said,

turning around and undoing the strap securing Lem down. Released, Lem floated into the middle of the ship's cabin in zero gravity. He laughed as he bobbed, turning slowly upside down.

The others quickly loosened their straps, joining Lem in floating around the cabin, giggling.

Lem swam over to the window and floated in front of it, sighing happily as he took in the incredible view of the universe from outer space.

Bobbing next to him, Chuck asked, "What do you think?"

"Such a big universe," Lem whispered awestruck. He glanced at Chuck and grinned. "I am definitely coming back here!"

"What?" General Grawl asked groggily, sitting up in his straps. "Where am I? Am I a zombie now?"

Everyone exchanged smiles at the general's confusion.

"This guy reads too many comic books," Skiff said, rolling his eyes.

Neera bumped into Lem as she shared his window. He pulled himself even closer to her. "Hey,

Neera," he said. "Now that this is all over, would you want to—"

"Yes," Neera replied.

Lem smiled. "You didn't hear what I was going to—"

Neera interrupted him with a kiss.

Lem would have felt as though he were floating in air . . . even if he wasn't already floating in zero gravity.

"Okay," Chuck said, climbing back into his seat. "Strap in, everyone; I'm taking you home."

Chuck turned the ship around and headed back toward the planet below.

Lem gazed out the window, staring at the whole world spread out like a map. As they got closer, his view narrowed to a vast stretch of desert, then to the suburban outskirts in a green valley, and finally to the park in the middle of town.

Chuck piloted the ship to a perfectly smooth landing in front of the town hall.

The townspeople gathered quickly and nervously approached. Police cars pulled up beside the ship;

and officers stepped out, aiming their guns at the alien lander. Chief Gorloc stood in front of his team, his gun aimed at the ship's hatch. A troop of soldiers who had remained in town hurried over, led by their chunky captain.

The hatch slid open and Lem stepped out, followed by Neera, Skiff, Eckle, and General Grawl. Finally, Chuck came out onto the town hall lawn.

The policemen shifted their aim, focusing right on Chuck.

"Look!" one man screamed, pointing at the astronaut.

A solider near the man screamed, "The monster!"

General Grawl spread his arms wide and stepped in front of Chuck. "It's all right, Chief," he told Gorloc. "He's with me."

When Chief Gorloc lowered his gun, General Grawl clicked his heels together. "Soldiers, attention!" he barked. "There is among us an *astronaut*!" He whirled around to face Chuck. "Captain," he said, "thank you for coming back for me." Then the general saluted Chuck sharply.

Chuck smiled and returned the salute. "A pleasure, General," he said. "Maybe next time you have guests, you'll throw a better party."

Lem's parents rushed out of the crowd and enveloped Lem in a tight hug. Neera and Eckle's parents were right behind them, hurrying to embrace Neera.

Chuck kneeled down next to Eckle. "Kid," he asked, "how would you like to be president of the local Chuck Baker fan club?"

Eckle nodded, beaming proudly. "Oh, yeah!" he cheered. "Chuck Baker rocks!"

Reaching into his space suit, Chuck pulled out a big stack of signed headshots and handed them over to Eckle with a flourish.

Chuck rose to his feet and noticed that Skiff was standing in the hatch entranceway, his hand on Rover's round head. "Rover," Chuck asked, "you coming or you want to stay here?"

With a whir, Rover tilted his head up to look at Chuck . . . and then shifted to focus his single eye on

Skiff. The robot nodded his head and leaned against Skiff's leg, buzzing with love.

Chuck smiled at Skiff. "He needs oil every so often . . . and a whole lot of love." The astronaut nodded at Rover. "See you, boy."

Hearing the decision that Rover could stay, Skiff jittered with happiness. He and Rover jumped around, dancing on the lawn.

As the throng of onlookers around the ship got more crowded, Chuck glanced down at his chest and read his digital readout—he had only a few minutes left. Quickly, he looked around to find Lem.

Across the crowd, Lem scanned the mob, searching for Chuck.

Their eyes met and they both smiled, hurrying toward each other.

When they were close together, Chuck said, "Lem, you saved my life."

Lem nodded happily. "You saved mine, too."

Neera appeared next to Lem, and he put his arm around her.

"Hey, take care of this guy, okay?" Chuck told Neera.

Neera smiled and nodded.

Then Chuck turned back to Lem and opened his arms. They hugged tightly.

As soon as he let go of Lem, Chuck headed for his spaceship. Before he entered the hatchway, he glanced back. "Hey!" he called. "You are a great planet! Your '50s are fine, but . . . give me a call when you get to the '60s, okay? Because that's going to be fun!"

Chuck stepped into his spaceship and the hatch closed.

Everyone backed away, giving the ship room to take off.

The ground rumbled as the ship headed back into outer space. The whole crowd of townspeople waved good-bye to the alien astronaut until the smoky trail of his ship had completely disappeared into the clouds above.

Lem let out a big, happy sigh, grinning as Neera tightened her hug around his waist. Their eyes met, and they shared their second kiss. It was just as wonderful as the first one, even if it wasn't while floating in zero gravity.

Watching them kiss, Skiff began to tear up. He pulled out a handkerchief and wiped his eyes.

Then he handed the handkerchief over to Rover, who took it in his claw. Rover dabbed at his own single eye. The little robot let out a mechanical whine that sounded like a satisfied sigh.